A Jewel in the Maldives

Katherine Bell

Merry Robin Publishing

For my husband, my forever favorite love story
And for Megan, for inspiring me to write this book

Contents

Chapter 1

Two weeks before Christmas, I was eating leftovers on my couch watching reruns of Matlock. Five days later, I was on a plane to the Maldives.

M y sister Cassandra had come over and saw me on the couch feeling sorry for myself. It was a few months after my divorce was finalized. I had a hard time feeling motivated to do anything. The divorce weighed on me, although I was glad it was finally over. It was a long time coming—the marriage had been on life support for years, but it took a surprising amount of time for everything to be finalized.

Cassandra, in her typical brisk way, said, "Tanna, it's time. You've spent enough time grieving. It's time to get up and do something for yourself. It's Christmas time: do something you've always dreamed of."

You wouldn't think that as a woman in my fifties, I'd need my big sister to look after me, but I did. It was the kick in the pants I needed. She told me to take a vacation. A real vacation. The kind of vacation I never did while I was married to Jeff.

My mind conjured up a memory of a little brochure at the bottom of my bedside table. I went and pulled it out. It was full of pictures of thatched bungalows over the water, relaxing waves, pristine beaches, fresh fruit bars, and vivid sunsets. My first view of the Maldives. My dream vacation.

I saw this brochure for the Maldives ten years ago, and I kept it. I asked Jeff at the time if he wanted to go, but he scoffed and said it looked like something for lazy people who want to rot in the sun. He saw the pictures of all of the food, and he said we would never go to a place like that. That much rich food would throw off his training. He was in the middle of his latest diet and workout regimen. This one had him waking up at 4am to work out and had something to do with eating a lot of cabbage. I was never able to eat cabbage after that.

I hid the brochure and dreamed about going someday. Jeff always preferred camping and mountain climbing. He used to drag me and the kids into the camper, and I'd spend a week dirty, getting eaten by mosquitoes and stressing about feeding everyone.

During those years of intense dieting and exercise, I never enjoyed food. It wasn't until after the separation that I rediscovered my love of food. I started a blog all about food that ended up going pretty viral. I wrote about my journey rediscovering my love of cooking and of food as a new middle-aged divorcee. I had a steady and loyal following, and it led to some interesting work reviewing restaurants and invitations to speak and write for different newspapers.

I received a decent amount of money in the divorce. Jeff wanted things to end as quickly and easily as possible. He said I could have what I wanted. I wanted the condo, and I wanted to have enough money so I did not have to worry about working full time. Although I had a little money coming in from the blog, it wasn't enough to solve my financial concerns entirely. Jeff had a lot of money through a trust set up by his grandfather. Jeff had never had to work a day in his life, although he tried his hand at almost any reckless quick money scheme that crossed his path.

After I learned about the affair (which didn't surprise me) and the amount of money in his account (which did), I named a price, worked it out with my lawyer, and got double what I wanted. After paying for all the legal fees and other outstanding debts, I still had some money left over. Not a lot, but enough that with some good budgeting and planning on my side, I had enough capital to take my dream trip to the Maldives.

What better time of the year to start things out fresh than over Christmas time? Besides, Christmas was my favorite time of year, and I didn't want to spend most of it alone in my house waiting for the celebrations with my family. I wanted to be in my happy place during the happiest time of year. And my happy place always consisted of sunny days on the beach and in the ocean surrounded by good food. I booked my trip so that I would be coming home Christmas Day.

Chapter 2

So after five days of planning, I booked a ten-day trip and was on a large plane heading to the Maldives. On the flight I fell asleep. In my dream, I looked at the sun sparkling on the water like little diamonds. I saw little bungalows built right over the water on stilts with their private water slides and swimming pools. I looked to my left and found myself captivated by a mysterious man, seated on a lawn chair. He had long legs. His body was tanned, smooth and sleek, and he had broad shoulders like an Olympic swimmer. His black hair sparked with streaks of silver. An open book rested on his lap.

I wanted to see his face. I squinted my eyes in the light trying to get a better look at his face, but his sunglasses obscured what I was sure were enchanting eyes.

I wanted him to turn to look at me. I felt it in my bones. A longing I hardly recognized. It wasn't a feeling I recognized, even when I was in love with Jeff, which was a long time ago. I felt butterflies flutter around my stomach as I watched his face and admired his herculean nose and chiseled cheekbones. It would be pure heaven to see his eyes, even more heavenly than digging my toes into the warm sand.

A bit of turbulence as we descended bounced me back into consciousness. But the memory of the dream lingered. Just thinking about that man, remembering how badly I wanted him to look at me made the tips of my fingers tingle. It felt like a premonition.

I always believed in fate and the Universe coming together to bring soulmates into the world. It didn't take long being married to Jeff before I knew it was hormones and not fate that brought us together in the first place. I stayed married to him because I never wanted to get divorced. My best friend's parents divorced when I was a teenager, and I swore I would never do that to my children. So when we had our first baby, I promised myself that no matter what, I would stick it out for them. It took me a good thirty years to square with myself and let go of that promise.

As we landed, I stretched my neck to see through the window, but all I could see was the back of the head of the guy at the window seat. No matter. I would have plenty of time to see the landscape during my stay. My stomach fluttered—maybe from the descent, maybe the anticipation at finally finishing the long day of travel, maybe from excitement at being in the Maldives, or maybe even from the memory of my dream man, whose image stayed in my mind's eye. In any case, I couldn't wipe the smile off of my face.

As we rolled to a stop and everyone started gathering their things, I bumped my head getting up from my seat. I looked around at the other passengers and smiled in embarrassment. I grabbed my backpack and other luggage from the overhead bin to exit the plane and smiled at the flight attendant as I passed by. "Enjoy your stay," she said. I assured her I would.

I took a taxi to my resort. I watched the ocean, transfixed the whole ride there. It's not like I had never seen the ocean before. But I'd never seen anything like this. I lived near the California coast for years, and the Pacific Ocean was never far away—another reason why my husband never believed in going to the beach for vacation.

So I'd spent a lot of time driving near a beach, but this was nothing like the California beachfront back home. The water was blue. Really blue. *Is that what cerulean looks like?* I wondered. The lush trees and the bungalows silhouetted against the ocean view. It was spectacular.

Chapter 3

The car pulled up to the resort, and my breath caught in my chest with glee. I was finally here. I wanted to scream my guts out as I looked through the big glass doors to the ocean view on the other side. I saw the overwater bungalows in living color, not on a printed brochure or a little icon on the internet. I would be staying in one of those! I walked through the doors and looked out over the view at the bungalows.

As much as I tried to stay in the moment, the details of my divorce invaded my thoughts like uninvited strangers breaking into my home. I wished I could share this moment with someone. I didn't really want Jeff here. I could imagine him complaining about the heat, but I felt a pang of loneliness, a loneliness I had tried to avoid by staying married.

At my core, I knew that I probably would have stayed married if I hadn't learned about the affair. I was embarrassed by that. Our marriage was over long before that, and I wish I had had the courage to stand up for myself and leave a long time ago. But I was too scared.

In the intricate dance of our marriage, there came a point where the role of spouse morphed into something unfamiliar, a subtle shift where compassion veered into caretaking, and it faded into one-sided nurturing. There wasn't any romance, and I began to notice that I was supporting him and taking care of his needs. I was more like a parent than a partner.

"Stop it," I said aloud, making a conscious effort to shift my attention back to the view before me. No more thinking about home, divorce, or what I left. My children were all I wanted to remember from home. My two beautiful girls are grown women now with families of their own. They were my reason to smile, my reason to be excited about life, and why I believed in more chances for happiness. They were my reason for coming home so I could share all my experiences from this vacation with them.

The ocean appeared as though it reached clear across the planet. Not a cloud in the sky, no wind, no rain, just sunshine lighting the earth and keeping the temperature at a perfect 82 degrees. I eyeballed the bungalow cottages from a distance and imagined a black mat with golden letters spelling the word "Welcome."

The overwater bungalows were perched wooden stilts a few feet above the ocean's surface. The walkways were made of wood and had old-fashioned English lanterns positioned carefully on each side, which I assumed would keep the walking tourist from taking an unexpected swim at night. The central walkway was positioned so there were bungalows on either side. Some bungalows had private swimming pools with slippery slides. Others had wooden step ladders leading directly into the ocean.

I walked slowly along the walkway toward where people were gathering to check in. Five buildings clustered close together near the end of the walkway. They buzzed with activity. I looked into the exercise room, at the ice cream stand, candy palace, lounging areas, business offices, and a kids' playroom. My plans formed quickly as I glanced into the food court on my way to the front desk. The food looked so beautiful. Stacks of fresh fruit, baked goods, bowls of salads and grilled meat created a panoply of color and smell. Some of the food was arranged to form sea creatures and other aquatic scenery. The set up would for sure win first place in a photo contest of *Taste of Home* magazine. I planned to check in, lug my baggage to my villa, and then walk directly to the food court. I was starving.

I entered the first building to find the registration line. The high vaulted ceilings were decorated with long transparent jellyfish, and three dolphins arched for a dive back into the water. The walls themselves were light aqua. The light reflected off the water outside and danced along the walls, creating an impression that we were underwater. The effect was enchanting.

As I waited in line, I pulled out all the necessary papers from my handbag so I could be checked in quickly. As I approached the desk, the lovely young woman behind the desk asked for my papers and ID. Her name tag said "Megan-Anise." How pretty. As she put in my information, I asked her about the activities I could book through the hotel. She gave me a pamphlet that outlined a variety of activities that required booking in advance including scuba diving (requires certification), snorkeling, paragliding, swimming with dolphins, sunrise yoga, and an underwater restaurant. I asked her how much a typical dinner cost at the restaurant. "On average, people spend about $300. You can spend a lot more depending on how much you drink. The food is very highly rated. Some of the best in this part of the world. The chef has won a lot of awards for his recipes and techniques."

"Oh right," I said, trying to sound cool, like $300 on one meal was not completely out of my budget.

I decided to book a snorkeling class for tomorrow. I would have liked to try scuba diving but I wasn't certified. The restaurant was what I really wanted to do more than anything, but there was no way I could fit that into my budget if I wanted to do anything else while I was here.

"Your snorkeling appointment will be at 10am tomorrow morning. The details of other activities will be sent to your room each day."

"Okay, thank you."

When everything appeared in order, Megan-Anise copied papers, and I signed two of them. She gave me a copy and my room key.

"Welcome to the Maldives. The dinner lounge is open for dinner at 5:00," she smiled and pointed to the right. I picked up my suitcase, backpack, and handbag—hopefully the last time for a long time. They felt like they were getting heavier by the minute as the very long travel day wore on. I was ready to lie down.

But clumsiness decided to strike right then. My red wallet hit the floor, sending pennies, dimes and quarters flying everywhere. Why do I still carry so much change? I froze. Everyone stared at me, my cheeks burned as I bent to pick up the money.

"We'll help you," came a chipper voice to my right. Two children from the line closest to me walked over and helped me pick up the coins.

When the last coin had been put back in my wallet, before securely zipping it shut, I pulled out two quarters and gave them one each. I was truly thankful for their help, especially that I didn't have to be scavenging on the floor all alone. I walked out of the registration building and headed for my room.

My room was called Mermaid Cove. A mosaic plaque with a mermaid on the door greeted me. She had shiny gold flowing hair that snaked around her body like the waves of the ocean. Her tail was made of light blue and shimmery mother of pearl. Seeing her made me consider joining her and her ocean friends for a swim. But first, I needed a shower, a change of clothes, and some food.

After opening the door, I stared at the room and all the furnishings. I dropped my luggage inside and put my hand over my mouth to stifle what would have been a loud "WOW" that would surely wake up anybody taking a siesta within a few feet of me.

The decor was cool rustic cream, light and welcoming. The suite had one huge bedroom with an equally large bathroom, a kitchen and a living room that opened onto a terrace compete with a private pool. There was no door to the patio, merely a sliding glass opening that enabled me to view the ocean. My feet led me right to the patio, which would be a gathering place if anyone came over. Looking at the blue water in my private pool, I knew intuitively that I would probably spend more time in it than anywhere else. I walked back inside and fell backward on the bed with white tightly tucked-in sheets.

With the windows open, I could feel the ocean breeze on my skin as though my room fan had been turned on low. I lay motionless, and my thoughts drifted to my clan back home. I wondered how everyone was doing. I thought of my own two daughters, Ruby and Betty and their little ones. I missed them so much but knew I would see them after my trip. I looked forward to finding Christmas presents in the Maldives that I could bring back.

I tried to call both of my daughters, but they didn't answer. Maybe later, I thought. I sniffed myself and decided to take a shower before going to the food court. I was so hungry I could have eaten an entire roasted pig, which I hoped was on the menu.

After luxuriating in the warm shower for longer than I intended, my stomach truly started to grumble. Not wanting to waste any more time, I decided to just touch up my makeup, throw my hair up, and slip on my new favorite ruby-sequin studded sandals before heading straight to dinner.

I grabbed my purse, made sure I had my room key, and the door automatically locked after shutting it. I walked down the boardwalk and turned right to get to the restaurant, all while seeing the bottom of the ocean beneath my feet through the cracks.

I could smell the food as I walked into the open-air restaurant. Prime rib was the dominant delicious smell.

The specialized chefs and artisan food makers were bustling around in their tall white chef hats and double-breasted white coats.

I got a Diet Coke and sipped it as I walked around and surveyed the food. I thought about the life I'd left behind. In all reality, it would have been easier to stay home, lay on the sofa with a soft fuzzy blanket nestled close to me, with the remote in one hand and a glass of wine in the other.

But no, my children would have disagreed with that. They were always telling me to "get out and do something," "meet new people," and "move on." They were proud of me for booking this trip. As I took a sip of my drink and walked past the dessert table, I thought, *don't you love how kids know exactly what is best for you?* You spend your whole existence thinking and planning for them, and as they get older, they seem to have all the answers on how you can fix your life. In this case, they were right.

Whether my kids knew it or not, I was trying to move forward in my turtle pace sort of way. I'm one of those people who struggle to take big leaps into the unknown, even when they might be good for me. Back home, after sitting in my front room night after night doing nothing, I took a baby step forward by booking this trip. One small step for man. One huge step for me. Cassandra told me to "get out of Dodge," and I did.

"Besides, Cassandra will be with you, so you will have a great time," Ruby had said. Cassandra said that she would come for the last few days of my trip so I wouldn't be alone for Christmas. I would have a few days here on my own first, and by the looks of things so far, I was going to have a wonderful time.

The food was beyond words, and I felt better now that I had a full stomach. As I pondered my life as I sat alone, I started to feel brave. I opted to kick divorce, insecurities, and scared feelings to the back of my mind where they belonged. I wish I could kick them out of my head altogether like a football flying past the end zone.

I switched my focus to my surroundings. How satisfying it was to sit in the food area on the patio and rest after a long day of traveling. I watched the other people in the food court. A couple families were finishing their meals, including the family with the two girls who helped me at reception. They saw me, and I waved. They waved back. They reminded me of my grandkids. Besides the families, there were many couples close to my age, probably empty nesters, too. And a few people sat on their own. A tall man sat with his back to me a few rows over reading a newspaper. He had bright orange socks on and sandals. *Huh*, I thought. *That's an interesting choice of footwear.*

I started to feel drowsy. My brain started getting a little fuzzy. I thought of my bed in the bungalow without me in it. Before I fell over, probably smashing my head on my plate and making a mess, I went to put my tray on the cart. I looked forward to hitting my head on those soft pillows and curling up in white sheets. I wondered if I would see those girls again or maybe the man with the orange socks.

Chapter 4

The next thing I knew, sunlight was streaming in through my window. I looked at my watch. It was almost 9am. I lay back down and closed my eyes. How long had it been since I slept in like this? I was fully awake with my eyes closed and heard a soft low growl. I smiled because I knew there was no angry animal in the room, only my growling stomach. You'd think after all that food, I would still be full from yesterday, but my body felt like I had fasted for days.

I changed into my beige shorts and a flower top and slid into flip-flops. I combed my hair and pulled my long bangs back, clasping them tight into a barrette, which had been a gift from my daughter.

As I approached the restaurant, I could smell the amazing array of breakfast food before I could see it. Coming late to breakfast had its advantages. The room was pretty much empty. I had my pick of almost any table. Even the terrace was unusually empty. I could see only one man sitting in the outside eating area holding up a newspaper. He looked so elegant sitting there sipping his coffee. I did a double take. He was the definition of tall, dark, and handsome. He had sunglasses on, and I could just see his profile, so I couldn't get a good look at his face. However, I had the funny feeling that I had seen him before.

I walked over to the buffet and selected a piece of coffee cake with a cinnamon and brown sugar layer in the middle. For my savory part of the meal, I added a breakfast casserole with sausage and eggs, hash browns on the side, with two strips of bacon. I walked outside with my tray of food.

I got a table where I could observe the man without him seeing me do it. I couldn't place him until I was halfway through my hash browns, and it suddenly hit me. *He looks just like the guy from my dream!* I thought with a jolt of excitement. His hair had greys streaking through it the exact same way. His hair was cut short on the sides and long on top. He wore a light linen shirt and boat shoes. His sports jacket was tailored. He had on an expensive-looking but tasteful gold watch. This guy looked like he had some money, but not in a show-off kind of way. He oozed quiet luxury. Suddenly he looked at his watch, got up, folded his newspaper, and headed out the door.

I felt a pang of disappointment as I watched him go. I hoped it wasn't his last day on the island. Maybe I would get to see him again. We were staying at the same resort after all.

I had a little time before my snorkeling excursion. I decided to see the famous underwater honeymoon suite and the underwater restaurant. I reached in my bag and opened the pamphlet Megan-Anise gave me at reception. I learned that twelve pod-type rooms were available to stay in at $3,000 to $6,000 per night. Some pods were $50,000 per night including a private boat and a personal chef. Holy cow! I read a note that said you had to be a guest in the rooms to be able to see them. I felt a sharp pang of disappointment. There was no way I would be able to see those rooms. I sent a plea to the Universe to make it possible for me someday. At least I could go look at the restaurant, even if I couldn't eat there.

I went to the information desk again. I inquired where the underwater restaurant was. The receptionist pointed to the left saying the restaurant was at the end of the boardwalk about 15 feet below the surface of the water.

I walked to the end of the long pier and into a room with an open door. It was a small octagonal-shaped room with windows on all five sides. Across the room, I could see the entrance to the stairway which led down under the water to the restaurant.

On display above the stairs was a rectangular piece of glass, depicting the 125 mm thickness of the glass walls of the restaurant, the hotel, and the staircase walls. Situated directly above the piece of monstrously thick glass was a warning sign, warning people with claustrophobia and for small children to stay with an adult at all times.

In that case, I was lucky, I didn't have either claustrophobia or a kiddo yanking on my arm. I was free and could run down the stairs, two steps at a time if I felt brave enough. I waited for a group of people to go ahead of me. I wanted to take my time. I took my first step on the cement stairway and grabbed hold of the rails which were on both sides. It was a circular spiral winding staircase with fluorescent lighting and windows every fifth stair. Out of the windows of the first five steps there was blue sky.

For the next five steps in my journey downward, I watched the windows closely while holding onto the handrail. Things were changing. Instead of a full blue sky, ocean water was on the bottom half, while blue sky was on the upper half of the window. After taking four more steps, a yellow fish swam by the window. Yes, it was an actual fish, and the yellow scales looked bright like someone was holding a fluorescent light to his iridescent scales.

I had imagined an elevator to get me to the underwater adventure, but this was spectacular. You start your journey above water and gradually submerge without getting so much as a drop of water on you. I silently gave kudos to those engineers and professional minds who had come up with such an engineering miracle. I loved it. It felt new and adventurous.

When I got to the bottom, I stood at the entrance of the most fabulous restaurant I had ever witnessed. It was a glass tube with thick glass walls. It reminded me of the aquarium back home where you could see marine life in all directions. There were a few people dining, a couple at one table and a single woman at another. Because it was an eating establishment, a host inquired if I would like to be seated.

"No, thank you. I'm just looking."

The host directed me to a viewing room for those who just wanted to have a look without eating. They had benches for seating along the walls of the aquarium and a long bench in the middle of the room. I sat on the bench in the middle so I could see both sides. The man from breakfast was there too. In fact, I was pretty sure it was the guy with the orange socks and sandals from last night! But he had changed into sensible footwear for today. He was tall, maybe six feet or so, watching the fish make their journey from one side of the glass dome to the other, right over our heads.

His eyes caught my gaze, and he pointed at two sharks swimming directly overhead. He gave me a friendly smile, which took my breath away. I nodded, raised my eyebrows, and smiled the most alluring smile I could muster. He had initiated contact! I hadn't realized I was open for romance, but after seeing this guy, I knew I was. My mind immediately started to race, imagining romantic scenarios. The Maldives would be a perfect setting for a romance of my own.

The magic was over all too soon. He stood up, watched another school of fish swim over our heads, and headed for the lighted exit sign. He raised his hand to gesture goodbye. I couldn't think of a way to keep him there, so I weakly lifted an arm in response. Oh, my Lord in Heaven above, he was beautiful. This was the third time I had seen this man, and my imagination was running wild. I needed to rein it in. I've always been a hopeless romantic, but my marriage and divorce gave me a heavy dose of reality. Maybe that's why I was always escaping into my imagination. I was open for something to happen with a handsome stranger while I was here, but I didn't want to rush into a fling. If a genuine connection happened, I would be thrilled.

I sat there for a few more minutes watching the sharks. I looked at my watch. Romance would have to wait. For now, I had a snorkeling lesson to get to.

Chapter 5

I had never snorkeled or even used scuba diving equipment before. I wanted to complete scuba diving certification before coming, but to complete your PADI, you need academic training requiring five confined water dives and four open water dives. I didn't have the chance to get certified before I left for my trip. I vowed that when I returned home that would do it.

I followed the signs and found my way to the snorkeling dock. Upon arriving, I waited in line like everyone else. There were four snorkeling guides who passed out fins, a properly fitted mask, and a snorkel. When it was my turn, I held onto the wooden bench to avoid falling while I tackled the awkward fins. Next I slid the elastic band of the mask around my head so it didn't pull my hair and placed it over my eyes.

When I was equipped and felt comfortable, I inched my way off the dock and into the water. I took a breath and put my head under the water. I breathed through the mouthpiece as I had been instructed. It was easy. The fins propelled me forward like a fish, and I swam along gracefully listening to my own breathing.

The world was completely different under the water. The sounds I could hear were muffled like hands had been placed over my ears. Colorful coral, plant life, and fish were everywhere. I was surrounded by life of all shapes, colors, and sizes. Crabs scuttled along the floor; schools of tiny fish darted around me, and a black eel poked its head out of a hole. I looked to my left, and I thought I saw a sea turtle in the distance. I swam in that direction to get a better look. An iridescent blue fish swam by my side. I reached out to touch it, but he darted out of reach. I used my fins to keep up with the fish, but he got away.

My goggles worked well under water, and on my way towards the turtle, I spotted a pair of gorgeous, muscular legs to my right. I looked in that direction, and I saw that a man was looking straight at me. He was wearing a snorkeling mask, but he smiled, and waved underwater, and I realized it was the man I kept running into. I tried to say hi, but all that came out was an air bubble. He pointed out in front of him, and I saw the sea turtle again. It had come remarkably close to us. I could see the distinct pattern and variety of colors of its shell and the details of its head and fins. It looked like a little old lady, full of wrinkles and smiling. I looked back over at the guy, nodded and gave a thumbs up.

I had only a few more minutes allotted to my swim time, so I made a wide curve and started heading back towards the dock. I continued to watch the bottom of the ocean floor when something grabbed my attention. An object rolled around in the sand. It glistened pink as the sunlight danced along the surface. I reached down to grab it, but it was too far. I held my breath and dove under and grabbed it. I kicked off the ground and came back up to the surface. It sparkled in my hand. Its surface was unpolished and pink. It looked like some kind of jewel, about the size of a quarter. I put it in the waistline of my high-rise polka-dot two-piece.

I looked up. The scuba instructor was waving at me to come in, for my turn was ending. I swam like a real fish to get back to the dock. I pulled myself out of the water and gave my mask to the instructor and thanked him. I threw my towel around my shoulders and squeezed the ends of my hair with it. I slipped my flip flops and cover up back on and headed back to my villa.

As I walked back to my villa, I wondered about the jewel I had found. I pulled it out of my swimming suit and examined it. It was very beautiful. I had a hard time imagining it was real. I could only imagine how it would shine when it had been polished. Where did it come from? I put it in the pocket of my cover up. I took the long way around the hotel and through the lobby for a little post-swim stroll. I stopped by the food court and grabbed an apple. Snorkeling had made me hungry.

As I ate it, I leaned against the railing and looked at the tropical view from the lobby. I listened to the wind rustle the leaves of the palm trees. I couldn't help thinking about this guy I kept running into. Would we ever officially meet? Would I ever learn his name? I was aching to know more about him.

When I walked around and reached my villa, I was about to put my keycard in the door when I noticed it was cracked open. I stood there in shock. Was someone here? I didn't see a housekeeping cart anywhere. I felt uneasy. I decided to play it safe, so I turned around and walked back onto the main boardwalk.

From where I was standing, I could see the front doors of each villa. Four villas away, a man was exiting his villa. It was my crush! Soon to be my knight in shining armor. He must have gone straight from the snorkeling session to his villa to change because he was in a loose button up and trousers. I, however, was still in my cover up and flip flops, my hair damp from swimming—certainly not the way I'd like to present myself for an official meeting. It didn't matter though. I needed someone's help. As a single woman, I wasn't taking any chances, and I needed someone to come check my room. I wasn't going to complain if it was him.

I waved at him. "Excuse me, sir, would you please help me?"

He looked over at me. "Of course. How can I help?" His voice was deep and warm. Like hot chocolate on a cold day. He came over to me.

"As I was going back to my room to change, I noticed that my villa door was already open, and I'm nervous to go in. I'm afraid someone might be in there."

"Is this one yours?" he asked.

"Yes, this one right here." I pointed and led the way to my villa. He looked at the door, paused for a moment, and cracked it open with his hand until he could see into the front room.

"Hello?" he called. "Is anyone there?" Then he opened the door all the way and stepped in. "Why don't you wait here while I look inside?" he said with a glance back at me.

I stood in the open doorway while he moved from room to room, calling as he went.

He called me in. "Come on in. I didn't find anyone. Does anything look out of place?"

I walked in, glanced around, went into all the rooms, looked in my luggage and the hotel safe where I had kept my passport. Everything looked the same as when I had left for my snorkeling lesson. "I think everything's fine. Nothing looks out of place."

He came out of the bedroom. I sat on the couch and pulled my feet up beneath me. He came and sat next to me on the chair.

"How are you feeling?" he asked.

"A little unsettled. I wish I knew what went on in here. Maybe it was a faulty lock, but I just have a strange feeling that someone was here." I kept having visions of shady figures creeping into my room and searching through my things. I was surprised how easy it was to be vulnerable with him—I didn't even know his name yet.

He reached over and touched my hand gently. "Everything is going to be okay. I will alert security about your door. It's best if someone from the hotel comes and takes a look at it just to be safe."

"Thank you. That sounds great." I looked over at the door distractedly.

"Do you want to wait at my suite while I go find someone and get this worked out?" he asked kindly. He must have seen the concern sketched on my face. And truthfully, I didn't want to be in my villa alone, so I agreed.

"Okay, if it isn't too much of a bother."

"No bother at all." His smile was comforting. He had one of those smiles that puts a person immediately at ease. He breathed professionalism and a calmness under pressure. I got up with him, and we walked out of my villa together.

"Thank you for all this," I said weakly as he shut my door behind us, and we walked together down the boardwalk to his place.

"It's no trouble. I am glad I could help."

"I didn't catch your name."

"I'm Anthony, but my friends call me Tony."

"Do I qualify as a friend?" I teased.

"You do now," he winked at me, and my heart skipped a beat. Maybe this whole break in wasn't such a bad thing after all.

"And who do I have the pleasure of meeting?"

"I'm Tanna."

"That's a beautiful name. Tanna. I've never heard that one before."

"Thanks, I like it." He opened his door and gestured gentle-manlike for me to go in ahead of him. Tony's room was similar to mine but larger. High canopied ceiling with a chandelier light fixture. Interesting glass-blown figurines adorned the tables and a bookshelf. There were a number of plush armchairs, a large comfy couch, and a big screen TV in the main room, and wicker patio furniture spread out across the terrace to the private pool. Large windows reached from the floor to ceiling to allow in all possible light and air. It was spacious and tidy. He motioned for me to sit down, and I sat in one of the armchairs and looked around to the view of the ocean.

Tony called security on his phone and explained the situation. When he finished, he let me know that they would send someone over right away. He told them that they could contact me in his villa once they had sorted out the new keycard.

Tony got up and went into the kitchenette. He opened the refrigerator and asked, "What would you like to drink? I have flavored water—lemon and berry—or orange juice, or a couple of Cherry Colas. What will it be?"

"Could I have a Cherry Coke? It's my favorite drink."

He laughed. "You can have two if you like." He handed me the cold can with a glass.

I sipped my drink. I liked how it burned slightly in my throat as it went down.

"I don't think I've thanked your properly for coming to my rescue."

"It was nothing. It was the least I could do."

I smiled and shrugged not really knowing what else to say. I was starting to feel a little more relaxed sitting at Tony's kitchen table, sipping my favorite drink. Trying not to be obvious, I checked him out. I glanced at his legs and flip-flops remembering how good they looked in the water this morning. I've always thought a man's legs were his most attractive feature, and man, those were the best legs I'd ever seen. I bit my lip to keep myself from grinning. I looked away as though I were checking out his villa.

Thankfully he broke the silence. "Where are you from?"

"I live in Belmont Shore, California."

"Belmont Shore, huh? Is that close to Long Beach?"

"Yes, it's between Long Beach and Huntington Beach."

"Does that mean you live in a beach house and the ocean is your backyard?" He gestured out the window.

"I wish." I smiled back. "No, my usual life is less romantic than this. I live in a condo about fifteen minutes from the beach. It's nothing special, but we do have a swimming pool."

"Oh, okay, I thought maybe you were one of those California surfer girls with a great tan and maybe a couple of tattoos."

"Nope." I extended my arm to him so he could see my lack of tan and tattoo, and we both laughed.

"I don't have a great tan. I'd love to be one of those surfer girls though, roller blading down the boardwalk in short cutoffs and a T-shirt."

"Yeah, I think that life appeals to a lot of people. Do you spend your days on the beach?"

"Actually, I have to work while the sun shines, but if I'm not too tired, I drive down to the beach, find a parking spot, and walk along the beach at sunset to see the sun grow smaller and fade into the ocean."

"That sounds nice. And what do you do for work?" Tony asked.

"I worked as an executive assistant for a long time, but a few years ago, I started keeping a blog online to document my love of food and to try out new recipes. I started to write reviews of my experience going to different restaurants in my area—this was before the days of Yelp and Google Reviews were as popular as they are now—and I got a pretty good following. About a year ago, I was taken on by my local newspaper to do a column once in a while as a guest. So I guess some people would call me a food critic. I just think I'm a normal person who likes food and likes to blog."

"That sounds like a dream job. What's your favorite part?"

"I get to eat a lot. Who doesn't love to eat good food? But also," I thought for a second, "I guess my favorite part is the community. I never realized how fulfilling it would be because of all the people I have met. Chefs, waiters, suppliers, busboys, other critics and foodies. I never thought the world of blogging and food reviews would expand my world so much."

"Did you study food science or something like that?"

"Actually no. I don't even know that much about food. I'm no expert or anything. I think people have liked reading my posts and reviews because I don't get very technical about it, but I talk to people who do get the science and art behind it. I am sort of the mediator. I get to talk to people all the time who went to school to learn how to do this stuff. Other people working with food never studied a day in their life, but they found their talent and love of food, and found work in that. Food brings people together. It's a great equalizer. Everyone needs food, and so much of our lives revolve around it."

"That's certainly true. How has the food been so far here in the Maldives?" he asked with a wry smile.

"It's excellent, but you don't need to write about food to know that."

"Are you planning on writing about your food experiences while you are here?"

"I might write something afterwards, but for now I am on an extended break. I decided to give being a food critic a rest while I'm out here. I just wanted to enjoy it without thinking about how I would describe it for my audience. Whether or not I write something formally for my blog, I'll write excellent reviews online for the resort food. It really makes a difference for these restaurants to have people write reviews online. I'm happy to report that everything has exceeded my wildest expectations. But enough about me." I was anxious to hear about him. "How about you? Where are you from?"

"My home is in Macon, Georgia. It's where I grew up, and I think of it as my home base. I've moved around a lot for work."

"What brought you here to the Maldives?" I asked.

"I did some work in Sri Lanka last week and had extra time, so I booked a villa here to celebrate Christmas away from home. I got here a couple days ago."

"I'm here for Christmas as well. Some people want snow and sleigh bells, but I prefer white sand over white snow. So what do you do for work?"

"I do contract work for the US government. I help people get their visas to come to America," he said. I waited for him to talk more about his occupation, but he asked me a question instead.

"What do you think of this place?" he asked. He was looking out the window.

"You better not get me started or we could be here a long time." He motioned for me to go on. "I haven't been here too long, but the stresses of life seem to melt away the more I dig my toes into the warm sand." He nodded. His look was attentive and agreeable. It encouraged me to continue. "This is the best place I've ever been for relaxation. The sunrise this morning and the sunset last night were like nothing I've ever experienced—and that's saying something because California sunsets are beautiful. There's so much to do here! I love that you can scuba, snorkel," I listed them off with my fingers, "eat fabulous food, drink exotic drinks, go to shows at night, go to exercise gyms, get your hair done, have a massage and of course, swim. I will never be able to do it all."

He nodded. "That's very true. But at least we can try."

I tried to pretend that I didn't immediately notice how he used "we" and wished desperately that he imagined doing any of this with me. I went on. "And then whoever grows tired of the water and wants a change from the ocean, then there is shopping. You can go on land and shop to your heart's content. I'm sure I will want to buy more than what will fit in my suitcases to take back on the airplane."

I knew I could keep talking as I was feeling chatty. He was such a good listener, and whenever he looked at me, he seemed to invite me to continue. I felt so comfortable talking with him. I had almost forgotten my unease from earlier.

He chuckled. "Absolutely," he said. "That certainly describes this place to a T. This seems like the perfect place to come if someone suffers from high blood pressure. It relaxes you down to the bone."

I felt like my blood pressure was lowered just talking with Tony in this wonderful setting, but then it spiked a little as his gaze turned toward me again, and my heart fluttered. His blue eyes were piercing. I wondered what he wanted to ask next.

"Are you married?" he asked. My heart hammered. This was it. The reveal. Maybe he would think less of me for being divorced. Or this would be the moment he would tell me he was happily married with six children and secure the likelihood that our little exchange would forever be purely platonic. But I didn't have time to answer because the doorbell rang.

"That must be security," said Tony. He got up to open the door. I walked behind him. A man in uniform with "Security" written in white block letters across his right pocket stood in the doorway.

The security officer turned to me. "Are you the lady who had questions about her door key?" I nodded.

"I checked your door and the key. I also checked your villa to make sure there was nobody in there and no damage was done. Your villa is safe. Here is your new door key."

"Thank you." I reached inside my purse, pulled out the old keycard and handed it to him. "Here's the original."

"Thank you for your help," said Tony courteously. The security officer nodded and left.

Tony and I went back inside. "Whew, that's a relief," I huffed as I sat back down. "I must not have shut the door completely when I left this morning. I'll make sure I check it twice from now on."

Tony looked thoughtful. "Just so you know, if ever you run into a situation like that or have any trouble at all, I am staying close by. If I'm around, I'll be happy to help." Little did he know that he was on the top of my list of people who I would call on to help me any day. This mystery man had gone from being a complete stranger to a confidant and a friend (and a crush) all in one day.

"Are you traveling with anyone else or are you alone?" he asked.

"My sister is supposed to come out and stay with me for a couple of days to celebrate Christmas together."

"That's nice. Does she have a family?"

"Yes she does, but her kids are grown and out of the house. Normally she goes to her daughter's house for Christmas, but we thought it would be fun to spend Christmas together in the Maldives."

"It sounds like you two are close."

"Oh yes. We are close now. We fought a lot when we were young, but now, she's my best friend."

"She sounds like a good sister," he concluded.

I wanted to make contact with him again. We were sitting so close. I thought I could thank him. But how could I do justice to the service he gave me? Maybe reach out and touch his arm? But I decided to avoid making this nice moment potentially very awkward. Rather, I said, "Thank you so much. I guess I better get back to my villa. Thanks for your help. It was nice talking to you."

I wondered if I should say anything else, like "Do you want to go to dinner with me?"

Instead I chickened out and simply said what I'm sure was unmemorable, "See you later. Bye."

As I got up to leave, he got up and walked me to the door. I knew he was watching me because I didn't hear his door close. But when I glanced back after I opened my door, he'd gone inside.

Chapter 6

The first thing I did after entering my villa with my new keycard was to flop on my bed. I couldn't stop thinking about Tony. It was sweet the way he had helped me, but there was something else. There was a protective gentle kindness like a soft blanket thrown over me when I was with him. Being in his presence, I felt a sense of belonging. I knew that sounded strange because I had just met him, but there was a familiarity about being with him that I couldn't explain. Almost like we had met before.

Was I making this up? Was I in the Maldives fairyland? Did everything here seem mystical and magical making it easy to fall in love?

No. There was something. I couldn't explain it. Tony was a man who was at ease with life and the world and made me feel that way too. He was confident, but not arrogant. When I was with him, I felt more at ease than I had ever felt with my ex-husband. Is that how love is supposed to feel? Or is it something else entirely?

I sat up straight in bed and put my head in my hands. I realized I hadn't asked him if he was married. He had started to ask me, but our conversation had been cut short because of the security guard. I made a mental promise that if I saw him again, I would ask him big questions like *How long are you staying in the Maldives? Do you believe in love at first sight? Are you married? Do you have children?* Things like that. If I was going to let myself have a crush on this guy, I needed to make sure he wasn't already taken.

Hopefully, I'd see him again. I felt sure I would because our villas were steps away from each other, and I had already seen him three times in one day. Plus, he said he was staying through Christmas, just like me. I was sure I would run into him again.

I curled up on my side, closed my eyes, and lay quiet.

I remembered the jewel and took it out from my pocket. The jewel was magnificent, not something you would find every day in the ocean. It had a beautiful light pink hue, was rough, and unpolished. I was hoping this beautiful gem was the heart of the ocean and would bring me great luck, riches, and make me famous. Oh, and a little more courage wouldn't hurt.

Opening the top drawer of my desk beside my bed, I laid it carefully on top of the Holy Bible. I took a shower to wash out the salt water from my hair and got changed into something more comfortable—a sundress and sandals. I put on a little make up and blow dried my hair. While I got ready, I thought about Tony, wondering what he was up to right now. Wondering what those strong hands would look like linked in mine. I was daydreaming like that when I felt my stomach growl. I looked at my watch. It was past one o'clock, and the buffet was only open until two! With all the excitement, I had forgotten to eat. I put thoughts of Tony on hold and headed for the lunch buffet. I didn't want to miss it.

Leaving the villa, I pulled on my door twice to make sure it was closed. With my beige sun hat and matching purse, I set out for the lunch buffet. It wasn't crowded because it was close to 2:00pm. Only the family of four I had seen at breakfast stood in line in front of me.

The salad bar offered makings for tacos, chips, salsa, guacamole, clam chowder, along with loaded baked potato soup and tomato bisque. Rolls, bread, and mini croissants were a perfect companion. I chose the tomato bisque so I could dunk my chunk of artisan bread with whipped butter into it. A separate bowl of watermelon, cantaloupe, grapes, blackberries, blueberries, and of course strawberries added color to my tray. With each meal there were choices for Maldivian food in the buffet line also.

I carefully placed my tray on the table for two, secretly hoping Tony would appear, and wandered back for Cherry Coke and ice water. I cherished every morsel I placed in my mouth. It was like tasting food for the first time. The savory and the sweet all delighted my senses of sight, smell, taste, and touch. I rolled a blackberry between my fingers—it was the plumpest one I had ever seen. I opened my mouth and tossed it in. I didn't have to follow a recipe, cook the food, or wash a single dish while I was here. I didn't have to critique the food, just enjoy it.

I heard some commotion from the family's table as some food spilled to the floor. I was pretty sure the two girls that had helped me pick up coins were the ones sitting at that table. The younger one with braids was on the floor picking up a bowl of spilled fruit.

The older girl, who was about nine years old, caught my attention as she pulled out some yellow string. It was a little thicker than yarn, and she was weaving it in and out of her fingers. "Put that string away until we go back to the villa. You need to eat before we go swimming with the dolphins," her father told her. She looked disappointed but stuffed the string back in her front pocket.

I sat back in my chair, lifted my drink to my lips, then alternately ate a small four-inch fruit pizza while crunching a couple of ice chunks. A wave of happiness rolled over me.

What a pleasant place I was sitting in. No problems to solve, no earth-shaking catastrophes, no issues to confront, if only my mind would not default to stuff back home. The only decision I had to make was whether to take the omelet with veggies or the scrambled eggs for breakfast and otherwise figure out what to do in between the fabulously cooked meals. It felt so wonderful.

I had decided to go shopping after lunch, which would require a short walk on the boardwalk and a quick boat ride. Hopefully there was still room on the boat, as no reservations were required. Instead of jumping off my chair and heading for the boardwalk, I sat and watched the servers gather the food from the long-serving tables. They placed plastic cling wrap over each tray of food and shuffled it into a four-tiered cart with wheels to take back to the kitchen.

The family who had been in the dining room with me finished their food and left the dining area. That left me to reminisce about the events of the morning. I thought of Tony again. Thinking of him gave me a pleasant sensation in my stomach like tiny butterflies. I thought about how he had been protective of me, and how this may be what I needed to bounce back fully into dating and into reality. The divorce had been hard on me. I came to the Maldives when I was feeling so tender. But I was feeling really good the last few days.

Would this gorgeous man decide to go shopping too? Probably not. He would probably go over to the astronomy viewing lab. I also wanted to go there before I left the islands, but for now, I set my sights on shopping for the afternoon. I took one last sip of my drink, grabbed my bag, and stood up. But I needed to change my shoes. After the stress of the day, I knew the walk in town would do me good, and it would be fun to take the boat to the Maldives town. Fresh ocean air was good for just about anything.

I arrived at my villa—thankfully the door was closed this time. I tried the keycard. It worked. Maybe I really had forgotten to close the door properly last time. After changing shoes, I was on my way to the shopping area. The sun beat down as I walked, but my wide-brimmed hat helped ward off the bright rays. Little beads of moisture had formed above my upper lip. I pulled a tissue from my purse and blotted my face careful to avoid smearing the makeup I'd applied.

After stepping off the boat, I spotted the Island Bazaar, an elegant European-style boutique. Later, I thought I would get my hair done at Le Cute. There were ladies walking around waiting for tourists, offering to braid hair for a small fee. I made it my goal to hit every shopping store in the Maldives touristy area before leaving if I could.

The shops sold colorful tropical fish, beach wear, toys and games for children, hats, snacks, and just about whatever else a tourist might need on vacation. When I packed clothes for the trip, I decided to pack lightly because I wanted to try and buy original items with exciting colors and designs made here in the Maldives. The women's section looked like a plethora of all the colors of the rainbow. I selected a black kimono with big bright flowers to wear over my swimsuit. I also selected a light blue top with spaghetti straps, made with lightweight soft fabric like it had just come out of the dryer, and a pair of tight-fitting leggings of the same color.

As I brought my chosen items to the counter, out of the corner of my eye, I noticed a small man was standing looking at me from behind the mannequin. I assumed he was from the Maldives. He didn't look like a tourist, and he didn't seem to be shopping. I didn't pay much attention to him, though he was watching me with his dark eyes.

I placed my card on the counter, and the salesclerk pointed to the visa machine. I inserted my card and then looked once again at the fellow behind the mannequin. If he thought he was well hidden, he wasn't fooling me for a second. I waited for him to move or do something. Why was he watching me? When he didn't move, I got the clerk's attention and pointed to the mannequin. When the clerk turned around to see the mannequin, the man suddenly ran for the exit as though trying to escape. The clerk and I watched him leave the store.

"What was that all about?" I asked the clerk. She shrugged.

I signed the receipt and thanked the clerk. A little unnerved, I decided to walk a few steps, then sit outside the shops. What did that man want? Why was he looking at me like that? I was merely a tourist in the Maldives like so many other people walking and shopping. I tried to dismiss it. But the uneasiness gave me a similar feeling I had experienced earlier with my front door.

Chapter 7

I sat outside the Island Bazaar for a few minutes, then window-shopped at three more stores. I wanted to window shop first and get a good sense of what I could get for my girls and grandchildren for Christmas.

I dropped in to Best Coffee Roasters for a quick cup. When I walked inside, I thought I had died and gone to fragrant coffee heaven. The baristas behind the counter were busily making fresh lattes with white flower and heart designs on top. I choose a simple latte with a white heart on top. The barista let me watch him make the heart design and looked at me with a smile as he started his masterpiece on the caramel-colored foam in my coffee. It looked so simple, but it would probably require many ruined lattes for me to pour the perfect heart or flower in the cream. I grabbed my latte and thanked him. I sat outside under a plain pink umbrella and sipped the warm drink.

I wanted to try all the best coffee. The thought of all the blended, iced, and cold brews made my mouth water.

I saw a poster for a bus and boat tour on a Dhoni. I read the description. It said it was a cruise on a fishing boat, where'd I imagined experiencing the ocean firsthand, with more snorkeling and seeing more wildlife. The tours I had seen included a bus tour, which would take us to visit the Maldivian way of life, with communities of people who did fishing and farming. The area we'd go was less centrally located, which meant less touristy, so you could see what life really looked like on the Maldives for people who live here.

Additionally, for all the tourists at the resort and on the island, there were drum shows, magic shows, dancers, and standup comedy. I wanted to do as much as I could. I doubted I could fit it all in in a week, but I was going to do my best.

I tossed my empty cup in the garbage can. It was time to go back to my bungalow. I had saved time to swim in my private pool before going to dinner.

I changed into my swimsuit and checked the phone for messages. There were none yet. My family was probably waiting for me to get settled, and we still had to figure out the time difference. Besides, they knew I wanted to rest, relax and avoid the telephone if possible.

I was excited to go swimming. I had always felt connected to the water, to the ocean especially. I had a lot of happy memories in the ocean with my family growing up. I remember spreading my grandmother's ashes in the ocean with my mother when I was little after she lost her mother. Maybe that's one reason why the ocean always felt like a mothering spirit to me. Healing and comforting. Of course dangerous if not taken seriously, but on the whole, life-giving. I felt like the ocean's whole purpose here in the

Maldives was to envelop and comfort me if I could only surrender to her power.

When I stepped into my private pool and watched the ocean lap the sides of my pool, my troubles melted away as the water surrounded me. I thought of my favorite line from my favorite book, *The Awakening*, "The voice of the sea speaks to the soul. The touch of the sea is sensuous, enfolding the body in its soft, close embrace." I too felt a special spiritual and physical acceptance from this beautiful body of water—as if it was meant only for me—though I knew many people loved and cherished their time being near the ocean. The author Kate Chopin was probably a kindred spirit that way.

I stepped back into my pool and heard footsteps on the boardwalk. I opened an eye out of curiosity to see if maybe Tony had come home. But no. It wasn't him. As I lay with my head on the edge of my pool facing my villa, I could see the backyards of my neighbors. Although there was a privacy barrier between each villa like a side fence, I could see the young girl waving frantically at me from her balcony.

"Hi!" she yelled. "Can I come over and swim in your pool?" She extended her arms and proceeded to doggie paddle in the air to make sure I understood what she wanted.

"Ask your mom and dad," I called out.

"I already did!"

"Okay, hold on, I'll let you in." She ran back inside her villa while I stepped out of the pool and threw my towel around my shoulders.

By the time I got to the front door, she was already standing in my doorway staring at my welcoming mermaid plaque.

"I live right over there." She pointed her finger in the direction of her bungalow. I nodded. "We saw you at lunch today." She was bubbling with youthful energy. Her long curly red hair reached to almost to her waist, and she was covered in freckles. She reminded me of little Anne Shirley.

"I saw you too and when you and your sister helped me pick up coins when I first arrived."

"Yep that was us," she answered proudly.

"My name is Tanna. What's yours?"

"Mine is Abbey," she said as she eased into the pool up to her neck.

"I like your name. Is that your mom and dad and sister with you?"

"Yeah. My dad won a trip from his office."

"How do you like it here?" I asked her.

"It's so fun. I don't want to go home."

I smiled. I knew the feeling.

"I see you brought some yellow string with you." We both looked at the string Abbey had dropped on the ground before she waded into the pool.

"What can you do with it?" I asked her.

"Well, I'm trying to do something called Jacob's Ladder, but I can't finish the ladder."

"Why not?" I asked.

"Well, because it's hard, and I can't figure out how to get my hands just right, and the string gets all messed up."

"How about we dry our hands off on the towel, and I can show you Jacob's Ladder?" I said. "I can help you finish it."

"You can do Jacob's Ladder?" Her hazel eyes grew wide with wonder.

"Yes, I can."

"Okay!" Abbey jumped up faster than a toddler running for candy to get me my towel. "Here." She handed the towel to me.

We both carefully dried our hands, making sure the towel didn't touch the water, and dried in-between each finger. Then I blew on my fingers and told her to do the same. If our fingers were damp, the string would stick to our fingers, and it would mess up Jacob's Ladder.

After we felt that our hands were sufficiently dry, I took the string in my hands and started the ladder. When I came to the part that puzzled her, I slowed down and showed it to her three times.

She took the string from me and fumbled the first try.

"Move the string slowly," I told her.

She did and after a few more attempts, with a squeal of excitement, she finished the ladder. She looked up at me beaming. "Congratulations! Your first completed Ladder." I told her to go and show her mom and dad and later I would show her other string tricks.

She jumped up and as she ran, she turned around and yelled, "Thank you!"

I smiled and waved. "You're welcome!"

I watched her go into my bungalow and out the front door. I turned my head in the direction of Tony's bungalow. To my surprise, Tony was on his terrace. He waved at me. I waved back, feeling a blush creep across my cheeks. Had he been watching me teach Abbey the string trick?

Chapter 8

The next day, I slept in. I had booked a long session at the spa that morning, so I didn't see Tony at all. I got a facial, a stone massage, and a pedicure. I wiggled my toes and admired their new pink coat—complete with a painted palm tree and jewel on the big toe.

After lunch, I went back to my room for another swim in my pool. I looked over at Tony's bungalow again, and I saw him once again on his terrace. He waved, and I waved in return. He pointed to himself and then pointed to my pool. I interpreted that to mean he wanted to come over for a swim. Of course I didn't have a problem with that. I waved him over. My heart started beating very quickly as I waited, calculating how long it would take him to walk from his bungalow to mine.

I hopped out of my pool, wrapped myself in my towel so I could open the door for him. I ran to my bathroom to see how my hair and no makeup face looked after a day at the spa. I was looking fresh and radiant, if I did say so myself. The joy of being here glowed through my whole body. Then I heard a knock at the door.

I ran to open the door and slipped a little on my wet feet right as I got there. Luckily I caught myself on the door, which opened as

I pulled. Tony must have heard me crash into the door because he was smiling as if something was funny.

"Are you okay? I thought I heard a crash."

"Oh that was just me. I slipped as I came to the door," I mumbled in embarrassment. "Anyway, hi! Welcome back. Come on in."

I motioned for him to come in. "Thanks," he said. "The place looks nice." He nodded as he took it all in. "You saw it yesterday," I reminded him.

"I know. I was just being polite." He turned to me and smirked. A thrill shot straight through me.

"Oh right," I laughed. "Want to come swimming?"

"I hope I'm dressed right for the occasion," he said motioning to his swimming trunks and flip flops.

We went out to the pool. I unwrapped myself from my towel, stepped in, and swam to the side. Tony sat down on the edge and dangled his feet just as Abbey had done yesterday.

"Are you related to that little girl?" he asked.

"What little girl?" I asked.

"The little girl I saw over here yesterday." So he had been watching. The thought made me smile.

"No, I just met her. She came over yesterday. She likes string tricks, so I taught her how to finish Jacob's Ladder. I plan on teaching her more once she's perfected Jacob's Ladder."

"String tricks, huh? I've never done any."

"Not even when you were little? They were very popular with the kids in my school when I was young."

"Nope. Never. Maybe you could teach me someday, if you could ever fit me in." Wow, he was teasing me. That was a good sign!

"I'll check my schedule and let you know when I can pencil you in," I responded in kind. I glanced down at his legs in the water. I wasn't thinking of string or tricks anymore. I sure hoped he was single and that this wasn't just some friendly fling.

I heard him say something. "Sorry, what was that?"

"I asked how's your key card working?"

"Oh good, yeah thanks," I replied.

He looked at the water. "What are you doing for dinner tonight?"

The question took me by surprise. There's nothing he could have said that would have pleased me more.

My surprise must have registered on my face because he quickly added, "Well unless you're married or have a boyfriend who you are going with." He raised his eyebrows. I guess that answered the question of if he wanted to just be friends. My stomach fluttered dangerously. I hoped I would be able to keep my calm. I had no idea I could respond this way at my age. I thought my days of thrills and crushes and butterflies were long behind me. But Tony was proving me otherwise.

"No, I don't have either a husband or a boyfriend."

"Then how about dinner tonight at the dinner court?" His face brightened.

Though I wanted to go with him, I couldn't if he were still attached to someone else.

"Before I say yes, I need to know a little more about you. How about you? Wife? Girlfriend? Will you bring them along?"

"Well." He waited for five seconds which seemed like a full minute.

I was getting nervous. What if he had a wife back home or a girlfriend? Was he about to admit that he was attached but wanted to have some Christmas romantic fling? Was he a player? I wanted to get to know him, but I was afraid suddenly of what I could find out.

Finally, he spoke. "I have neither. I once had a wife, but not anymore." He shrugged and smiled at me. My whole body seemed to breathe a sigh of relief.

"Then, yes. Food court it is."

"How about a swim in your pool before dinner?" he said as he pulled off his T-shirt. I didn't say a word. I just stared at him. He was strong, muscular. His body moved with grace and precision, and with the dexterity of someone with fewer grey hairs. I saw the muscles of his arms flex as he lifted himself up. Tony obviously took care of himself. I hoped I wasn't a disappointment in comparison. I certainly wasn't bad looking, but I wasn't sure I oozed the strength and dexterity of youth the same way he did.

He headed straight for the pool slide, climbed all the way to the top, and as he slid down, raised his hands like he was a thir-teen-year-old speeding along on a roller coaster. When he popped out of the water and came up for air, he swam over to me and tapped me on the shoulder.

"You're it!" He darted to the other end of the swimming pool, then dove over the edge and into the ocean. I followed him, but I couldn't keep up with his Olympic-style swim strokes with my doggie paddle. But that wasn't going to deter me. I had another plan in mind. I moved closer to him but pretended I had lost interest in the game and looked at the big ocean all the while keeping him in my peripheral vision. As he did the backstroke with his eyes closed, I grabbed his foot.

"You're it!" I swam for my life with my head under the water to reach my pool and managed to climb over the side before he caught me. We both laughed. He probably let me win, but I didn't look back to see how close he was.

Tony climbed into the pool after me. We sat on the steps of my pool with our eyes closed, our bodies halfway in the water, and our arms floating. I liked Tony. A lot. He was fun, and I felt lighthearted when I was with him. His sense of humor was contagious, and it seemed to get me out of any serious thinking. And because he had helped me with my keycard, I felt like he would protect me.

I wanted to get us talking again. "So Tony, tell me something about yourself that not many people know."

"Hmm, let me think." I waited patiently while he thought. "Not very many people know my middle name."

"Really? What is it?"

He turned to me with a mischievous smile. "Do you want to guess it?"

"What? Are we in middle school or something?" I chuckled.

"Why don't we make a game of it? I can give you clues, and you try to guess it," he suggested. I felt like I was back in sixth grade, but I liked it. It felt fun and playful. "Okay, I'm game." Besides, how could I say no to those blue eyes?

"You are a good sport."

I put on my best thinking cap. "Okay, Tony, what's the first clue?"

"It starts with an S."

"Well, that narrows it down." I laughed. "Are you aware that if I guess your middle name, I will want a reward?" I wanted to lean into the playfulness of his personality.

Tony looked pleased. "Okay, what reward have you picked for guessing my middle name?"

"Something small, Tony. Just your firstborn." I smirked. Maybe I'm not that good at playful banter, but he laughed at my joke anyway.

"Wait, that sounds familiar, like the same trick that little man in the forest pulled. What's his name? Was it Rumpelstiltskin?" he asked.

"Yes, sir, it was indeed."

"So you're pulling the Rumpelstiltskin card?"

"Well, yes, that's where I got the idea. It worked for him so I figured it would work for me too. He was a smart little goblin." He laughed again. It was music to my ears. I felt the pull inside my stomach again. It felt like the tug of a fishing line. I giggled, too.

I lifted my fingers out of the water and noticed that they were starting to look like pale raisins. I told him I needed to call my daughters and apologized for cutting things short. He jumped up and lent his hand to help pull me out. This was the first time he held my hand—even if just for a second. More feel-goods pumped through me. I walked him to the door.

"I'll meet you back here at six," he said.

I closed the door and bit my lip in excitement. I felt like a school girl with her first crush again. Even with Jeff, it was never like this. All the fun and games. I wasn't very good at the banter thing, but with Tony, I never felt embarrassed. He laughed at my jokes and took me just as I was. This vacation was turning out to be quite the romantic episode. I'd read about this in books, but I never experienced it for myself. It felt too good to be true, but here I was, getting ready for a first date in the most beautiful place in the world.

I called my girls on a group call and talked with my grandchildren. It was the first time I had been able to get in touch since I left. I told them all about Tony.

"Wow, Mom, it sounds like a Hallmark movie. A Christmas romance in the Maldives."

"I know!"

"You deserve to have some fun."

"So you don't mind if I pursue a little romance while I am here?"

"Of course not! You haven't had any romance for a long time. Who knows, maybe this guy could turn out to be someone special."

"I think you are right." I told them I loved them and had to go. We arranged to call again in a few days. I promised the grandkids that I'd bring them something back from the Maldives.

I was a little surprised that my girls were so open to the idea of me dating this man I had only just met. But I guess we were a family of romantic hearts. We always spent the holidays watching these whirlwind rom coms set in gorgeous locations, and this was the first time I was experiencing my own.

I couldn't wait to meet Tony for dinner.

After I hung up with my girls, I went to take a bath. I needed to wash the pool and salt water out of my hair, and I wanted to make sure I smelled nice for my date. I just hoped that when Tony came to pick me up, my fingers resembled human fingers and not shriveled fruit.

I lay in my luxurious bathtub big enough for two with vanilla-scented bath balls. I kicked the bath balls under the running water to get enough bubbles to cover my body and head. I held up my arms and clusters of bubbles clung to them with aqua blues and greens. I leaned my head back and closed my eyes. I took deep breaths and listened to the sound of my own breathing. I could have stayed that way for hours. I knew I would fall asleep if I stayed too long. So after I washed my hair, I hopped out and proceeded to the shower to rinse off.

I sang "What a Wonderful World" as I got out of my shower, wrapped up in a plush towel and started to get ready. I blow-dried my hair and put it up in a clip. I dressed in the nicest dress I'd brought, a red floral gown with a deep V-neck and a lace trim. To finish off the look, I applied light makeup and a pretty rose gold lipstick.

I still had a little while before I expected Tony. I flipped through the channels on the TV and happened to come across one of my favorite black and white movies called *The Uninvited* starring Ray Milland. What caught my attention was the beautiful music called "Stella by Starlight." In the movie, Ray Milland wrote this song and played it on the piano for his girlfriend in a beautiful seaside cottage on a cliff in England.

I lost track of time, and before I knew it, the doorbell rang. I went to open the door, and Tony stood in the doorway looking like a god from Mount Olympus. I could have asked him to turn sideways and go all gaga from staring at his profile. But I didn't.

"Are you ready, my lady?" he asked politely.

"I am." I flipped off the black-and-white movie, grabbing my purse.

"You look beautiful."

"Thank you. You look great, too." And I meant it. That being said, I had never seen him when he didn't look good.

As we walked together toward the food court, I once again had that feeling of familiarity. I felt as though I was experiencing déjà vu. The thing that puzzled me was where it came from. Had I known him in a past life or something?

"Hey, Tony, have we met before?" It was a question I hadn't planned on asking, but it popped out of my mouth. It surprised me as much as it did him.

He turned and looked at me. "Well, not that I know of. I think I would have remembered you."

"Yeah, I would have remembered you, too. I just wondered."

When we arrived at the food court, there was no door to open, so he extended his hand, and I walked in first.

Standing in line it was easy to spot Abbey, her sister, and her parents. Abbey had her yellow string wound around her fingers and was staring at it intently. She looked up and spotted us. She waved and broke free from her place in line with her parents and skipped over to us.

"Hi, Tanna!"

She stared at Tony until I said, "Hi Abbey. This is Tony."

"Hi." Tony smiled at her, and she smiled back. From her wide excited eyes and her dancing feet, I could tell she was itching to talk about Jacob's Ladder.

"How's Jacob's Ladder coming?" I asked.

"Want to see? I can do it now." I could see by the look on Tony's face that he'd like nothing better. It was endearing.

Abbey proceeded to unwind her fingers from the yellow string when her parents started to scan the crowd to find their missing daughter. "She's over there." Her little sister shouted and pointed at us. Abbey's mom got out of line and came over for Abbey. "Hi. I'm Sarah." She looked at Abbey. "I hope you aren't being a nuisance."

"Oh no." I said. "I've been teaching her how to finish Jacob's Ladder, and she was just showing me how far along she is. I guess we are string trick buddies."

Abbey pleaded, "Can I stay in line with Tanna and Tony until we get up to the food?" Abbey pleaded.

Sarah looked at us. "Is that okay?"

"Sure, it's no problem," I said.

For the next few minutes, Abbey showed us the progress she had made with Jacob's Ladder and some other tricks she'd been working on. She had the tricks down pat. I told her that there was a way to play together, and each of us took a turn. I promised her that I would show her a magic trick and a parachute. By that time, Abbey's dad waved for her to come up and get food with them. She said thanks and waved goodbye.

I liked Abbey, but I was grateful to have Tony to myself again.

When we got to the front of the line, Tony and I gathered up two trays of delicious food. When we got to the register, Tony pulled out a heavy-duty credit card and paid for our dinner.

We found an out-of-the-way table for two. Tony went back to get the drinks. I removed the trays, buttered a roll, and waited for Tony to return. We dined on lobster with drawn butter, prime rib with a dollop of horseradish and a little au jus, kale salad with a creamy pecan dressing, and roshi, which is similar to a Mexican tortilla, cut in triangles. For dessert, we selected a local specialty, Maldivian sweetened condensed milk cake with large blueberries and a dollop of lightly sweetened whipped cream.

When we first sat down to eat, I waited for that gorgeous smile, and I got it when he took his first bite. The prime rib was cooked to perfection. There wasn't much conversation during those first few bites. I was playing with my lobster tail, cracking and digging at those hard-to-get pieces. I dipped them in warm butter and savored every mouthful.

I looked up at Tony. "I found something today."

"Oh really? What?" he asked with interest.

"When I was snorkeling, I saw it. I thought it might just be a rock, but when I picked it up, it looked like something special. It wasn't just a pretty pink stone. It looked like a jewel."

"That's interesting. What did you do with it?"

"I brought it back to my villa and stashed it for safekeeping in the top drawer of my desk. When I was in town, I noticed a jeweler's shop. I thought I might take it into town tomorrow and get the jeweler's opinion."

"Can I see it?"

"Well, yeah, if you don't steal it," I winked.

He held up both hands palms facing me, looking innocent.

"Do you really think it has some value?" he asked.

"I don't know, but maybe. When we finish eating, let's go to my place, and I'll show you. You will be the first person I've shown it to." I was excited to have someone I could share this with and grateful for his genuine curiosity. I had been wanting to share my thoughts about it with someone ever since I found it.

"What do you want to do with it?" he inquired.

"I don't know. I think it would be beautiful once it's polished. I thought of taking it to the jeweler and having some jewelry made. Maybe a pair of earrings or maybe a jewel for my navel," I teased.

I watched for his reaction to my jewel in the navel suggestion. He raised his eyebrows and waited for a few seconds. "Pink jewel in the navel huh? It's a nice visual. I'm sure it would look great. Would that be a new one for you?"

"Yeah, I've never done something like that before, but my kids would love it. You know what they say, 'What happens in the Maldives stays in the Maldives.'"

We both laughed.

We finished our cream cake and got up to leave. Abbey and her family had already left the eating area. Walking out to the boardwalk, our hands brushed. The sun had set. It would have been a perfect time for him to reach over and hold my hand, but we remained separate. He acted like he was having a fun time. I was shouting cheers in my heart that I was with him.

"How about a walk after we see the Hope Diamond in your villa?" There was nothing I wanted more than to continue to be with him whatever we did, but instead of divulging my true feelings I simply nodded.

We walked to my villa. I opened the door and turned on the lights.

"Hold on just a second, I will go get it." Tony sat at my kitchen table. I walked over to the bedroom, opened the top drawer, and pulled out the gemstone. I smoothed the rough edges with my finger, but it didn't do anything. I went into the kitchen and handed it over to Tony.

"Wow." He took the gemstone carefully in his hand and moved it in different directions to let the light shine through. "That really is something. I don't think this is just a common rock from the ocean."

"You think?" I laughed too.

"Do you think it is originally from the ocean or could someone have dropped it? I mean, jewels like this aren't usually something you find on a seabed. They are usually in mines, aren't they?"

"I have no clue where it came from. It doesn't look like a typical oceanic rock, and it isn't coral. I think you are right—it probably came from a mine. I would like to know the story behind it."

"Why don't we grab the gem, get on our horses and ride off into the sunset and not tell anybody?"

I laughed again. "You think I haven't thought of that?"

Tony handed the gemstone back to me. "That's a gorgeous gem," he said. "I think it's a good idea to take it to the jeweler and see if you can get it polished and learn the history of it."

I put the jewel back in the drawer on top of the Bible and wandered to the vacant chair.

"Now, I don't know much about you, except you have a semi-precious gemstone in your possession. You want to tell me about yourself?" he asked.

"What do you want to know?"

"I know a subject we can get started on—your kids. You can tell me their names, ages, and whatever else you want to tell me about them."

"Okay, that's easy," I said. "I have two girls. They are the loves of my life. Their names are Ruby Faye and Betty June. Ruby is a lawyer in Los Angeles, and Betty is a veterinarian in Denver."

"Do you have any grandkids?"

"Yes, I have four. Ruby has two beautiful boys. Their names are Ben and Ryker. Betty June's two girls are named Vivian and Eris. How about you?"

"Hold on a second. I gather you are single. Are you widowed? Divorced? What brings you to the Maldives on your own at Christmas time? Care to say anything about that?"

"I'm divorced, but can we postpone talking about exes and stay on the happy topic of grandkids for a little bit longer? This is our first date after all." I wanted to share with Tony, but I wasn't ready to get into the divorce yet. Plus, it left us plenty to talk about for a second date.

"I get the picture," he laughed. We talked some more about my kids, what they were doing, and some of their accomplishments. I thought to offer him some coffee, but upon inspection, my room didn't have any coffee. I tried to ask him about his family. But he seemed to read my mind.

"I also want to know about your parents and everything, Tanna. But before we talk about them and my family back home, how about we mosey on over to my place and sip of coffee or hot chocolate and munch on cookies?"

"Yeah, good idea. Let's get out of here."

When we arrived at his villa, he asked if I would like to come inside and watch him make the coffee or sit outside with the moon shining on the silver shimmery waves. I choose to stay outside with the moon for company. There was a stillness and calmness about the scene before me as I sat on Tony's deck, looking out at his pool and the ocean.

The moon looked almost full. It shined on the water, and the little glistening ripples calmed my wildly beating heart. I could watch it forever, wondering which ripple my eyes would follow next as new ones replaced the old ones. I heard the kettle start to boil. Tony bustled in the kitchen for a couple minutes and then he came out carrying a serving tray.

"Is instant coffee okay?" he asked from the doorway.

"Sure." I watched him carry the tray and come outside to join me.

Tony's place was apparently fully equipped. Glancing over the goodies on the tray, I saw two mugs, two spoons, two packs of instant coffee, cream, and Belgian Christmas cookies. I poured the coffee packet into my mug of hot water and watched it make caramel-colored bubbles. I added a little cream but no sugar because the cookies would be sweet. We sipped our coffee and munched on chocolate-covered cookies. I wanted to bask in the magic spell of the moonlight glistening on the water.

"So you were going to tell me about your mom and dad," Tony gently prodded.

"Oh yeah, right. They still live in our childhood home. My dad is a man for all seasons and reads *The Great Books of the Western World*."

"What's that?" Tony interjected.

"It's a series of books published by the Encyclopedia Britannica a long time ago as the essential reading for 'learned men.' It sits on our bookshelf at home. It includes books on Greek philosophy, and a lot of classic books of American and British literature. He's a professor at a local university back home, and he always valued our education. He tried to keep us kids up on every subject. I attribute my love of books to him."

"And your mother?"

"My mom was a stay-at-home mom and did a great job. She's a real southern belle. Being from Alabama, she introduced us to fried okra, savory corn bread with honey butter. We dined on crispy fried chicken and chocolate cake with a half inch of chocolate icing. But her banana pudding was the prize. She was the more religious one of the two. She read scriptures sometimes. Sometimes when we used the bathroom after her, the Bible would be open, sitting on the edge of the bathtub with red pencil covering the verses that were important to her. My dad also left his book in the bathroom. It was usually a self-help book. I can't remember the name of my favorite one, but I'll never forget the author's name: Karen Horney," I giggled.

"Interesting author name," he chuckled. "How did your parents meet?"

"My dad had traveled to Alabama. They were introduced at a dance, but my mom's dance card was all full, so my dad didn't have a chance to dance with her. But he remembered her. One day he was shopping in a supermarket, and he was sure the beautiful brunette ordering meat from the butcher was that same girl he had seen at the dance. He continued to watch her from the potato chip isle until she picked up her white taped package.

"He turned away, so she wouldn't see him, but a distinct impression came to him. 'I'm going to marry that girl,' he whispered quietly. And he did.

"He took her to California. Part of the time he was in the army. My sister, their first daughter, was born in Fort Sill, Oklahoma. Then their permanent home became California. My dad's parents lived within walking distance. My grandparents owned a little farm and one of my sisters or myself would walk to their place with an empty glass gallon, and it would be replaced by one full of cow's milk." I prattled on. I realized I had been talking for a while. Tony looked so interested and nodded in all the right places to keep me going. He was such a good listener. Jeff would have been on his phone checking his sports news by now.

I talked about my childhood, going to school, playing with cousins who would visit, and my mom yelling at me, "Tanna get in there and practice your piano, it's your turn."

"So you play the piano?" Tony asked.

"When we were kids, my sisters excelled on the piano and obeyed my mom's commands to practice better than I did. The very thought of practicing sent me to the piano with a huff of, *well if I have to.* My piano practice consisted mostly goofing off while sitting there, just to put my time in. Just as long as my mom could hear sounds from the piano, I knew I was safe and wouldn't get yelled at. I think my mother finally realized my heart wasn't in it. So after I had learned the basics, I was allowed to quit piano lessons much to my happiness.

"As my children were growing up, we had a piano," I continued. "Interesting how not having the piano teacher and my mother breathing down my neck, I bought some of my favorite music and started practicing on my own. Also I learned a new method from my friend Robyn of teaching myself chords and playing and assembling them into songs. There were books for this method and I bought a few to get started. The enjoyment I experienced as an adult in piano paid off. Now I play the piano in two assisted living centers for entertainment and in a hotel lobby. Occasionally, I am contacted by hospice to play for the elderly in their homes. My only hope when I play is that those who listen will experience peace and calm and a sense of wellbeing, that as long as they listen, their hearts will feel healing."

"So your mother got her wish after all. You have become a great pianist. And you bring joy to other people with your playing. I think that's beautiful. How did your mom like living in California? Did she ever miss Alabama?"

"I think she liked it well enough. But I know she always kept a strong sense of identity as someone from the South." Tony nodded as if he could relate. "But after a few years, she lost her southern drawl or maybe she intentionally let it go and learned to speak like folks from the west. I still smile when I think of her Alabama relatives coming to visit. My oldest sister and I would sit on the sofa trying to stay out of the way. As our southern relatives greeted our mom and they shared hugs, smiles and lost time together, we noticed a change in our mother's voice. We listened to her voice change with them. It magically took on a southern drawl we had never heard from her before. That side wasn't something we were used to seeing, but being around her folk from her childhood brought out the sweetness she used to experience with them."

"And what about your father?"

"My dad loved the Earth and wanted to make sure we all were aware of this planet. If we were on a trip, he would yell to the back seat, 'Stop staring at the floor and look out at that Morrison Formation. There could be dinosaur bones in there.' More than once he woke up everybody up at 3:00 A.M. to go outside and see the lunar eclipse that was happening *right now*. His passion for the world, for literature, for everything was infectious, but it was also a little oppressive at times. I won't say I was always a good sport about waking up early in the morning to see another comet. But I am grateful to him for all of that now." I paused, a little embarrassed how much I had talked about myself. I decided to turn the conversation to Tony.

"We've talked a lot about my family. Tell me about yours," I prodded. "Do you have children?"

He smiled. "Yes, I have two. They are wonderful people. Nobody robbed a bank or stole a car or anything."

"Then they are model citizens." I said.

"I'd say so. Their names are Finn and Evelyn."

"And where do they live?"

"They both live in Georgia, near home. They are both married. Finn works for the bank in town, and Evee works in real estate."

"Grandkids?"

"Yes, I have four also. Finn and his wife Amanda named their daughter Rue, and his boy he named Archie. Evee and Wesley have two girls called Coco and Rivi Nyx."

"Those are some very pretty names. Unique, too. I haven't heard of them before, I don't think. I like how kids these days think outside the box with names. I always liked having a unique name myself. I've never met another Tanna. I never had to worry about someone having the same name in my class, although I did have a Janna in my class once."

"Yeah, there are pros and cons to having a unique name. I always liked my middle name that I went by, but when I got older, I made the switch to Tony. It sounded cooler to me then. Sometimes I wish I hadn't, because I like that my middle name connected me to my grandfather. But Tony works well, too, and people have an easier time catching on when I introduce myself."

He paused for a moment. "When they named their first girl Coco, someone said, 'well that's not a name.' When Evelyn heard that, she said, 'Well, tell that to Coco Chanel.' I love that girl. She's got spunk."

That made me laugh. "That sounds like my daughter Betty." I smiled and sighed. I missed my girls. "What about your parents?"

"My parents are in their late 70's and are doing well. They are still healthy. They sold our childhood home, which was getting too big to ramble around in, and bought a condo with two bedrooms. My dad doesn't miss mowing lawns at all. My mom loved to garden and tend to her flowers, but as time wore on, the garden became too much. They told me their next move was going to be to a really fancy assisted living center where the establishment cooked all the food. That sounds great, huh? After they visited my mom's sister in one of them, they raved about how nice the independent living areas were. They said, and I quote: 'You can't believe all the activities they have there.' Dancing, drama club, tennis, a swimming pool, they are so excited. They apparently have a beauty parlor, and a podiatrist even comes regularly to trim everyone's toenails, if they want it."

"Wow, that sounds great for them. And what about siblings? Do you have any?"

"I have one baby sister. Her name's Mandy. I had to take care of her many times over the years. When we were young, she was always getting into trouble of various kinds. Nothing major, but juvenile stuff. I sort of became her protector. She didn't like that—she thought I was overprotective—and she tried to sneak out sometimes. I got good at sneaking around, too. I didn't want her to know I was watching out for her. Despite her rebellious stage, she grew up, and she turned out great. In fact, she got married to a nice guy named Gary, and they have three kids. There was a time when I thought that would never happen, but it did, and I couldn't be happier for her. She's a grandma too now. She just had her first. A little boy, Samuel. He is her whole world."

When I thought about my marriage, I was a little jealous that I hadn't felt that protection from my ex-husband like Tony had been to Mandy. Somehow, I felt I always had to be the protector, but it sure would have been nice to have that safe and *at home feeling*. I wondered if I was drawn to Tony partly because I knew he would protect me.

"Thanks for telling me about your family. Speaking of names of our kids and grandkids, what was your grandfather's name?"

He stopped abruptly. I was hoping he would slip and tell me, but his brow furrowed, and he caught himself before saying another word.

"Okay, that was a clever way to try to get vital information out of me, but no cigar."

I turned my head, "Darn," I muttered under my breath. "Could you at least give me another clue?" I tried again giving him my biggest doe eyes and batting my eyelashes.

"Yes, ma'am. I will give you another clue." He counted on his fingers a couple times.

"There are seven letters in my middle name. That's all the clues for tonight."

I held up my fingers and did the same thing raising each finger as I spelled *Samuel*.

"Wait." I said. "Samuel is your sister's grandson's name. I thought maybe he was named after you, but Samuel only has six letters. Unless you spell it with two Ls or something?" I asked hopefully.

"Nope, although I'm glad to know you were paying attention," he winked at me.

My coffee was starting to cool down, but I continued to hold the cup with both hands.

"I will have to keep thinking," I said.

He continued our previous conversation. "I heard about your kids, how about you tell me more about you. Where did you grow up?"

"I live in the big city now, but I am a true country girl at heart. I grew up in a small town in California back in the 60's and 70's. By small, I mean three girls in my graduating class and ten boys. Life was wonderfully simple in those days."

"Tell me about a memory you have of back then," he prodded.

"Okay. Let me see. Well, my playmates were my cousins and sisters. One fond memory of mine was when we were in elementary school. We waited anxiously for the bell to ring for recess, then waited again for all the kids to file out of the classroom and onto the playground. The record player was already set up on a table in the back of the classroom. My cousins and I raced to the back of the classroom, grabbed our favorite record, put the needle to the beginning of the record and danced the jitterbug. When the song ended, we flipped it over and danced to the music on the second side. We liked 'You Ain't Nothing but a Hound Dog' by Elvis Presley because it had a great beat and was easy to dance to. Another favorite was 'Wouldn't it be Nice" by the Beach Boys. Of course, any rock and roll song would do for us to dance to."

"I loved dancing to records in those days, although I don't remember ever doing it at school. What was another of your favorite songs?"

"Oh there were so many. We loved dancing to, '1 o'clock, 2 o'clock, 3 o'clock Rock', you know 'Rock around the Clock'?"

"Yup I know that one. By Bill Haley and His Comets."

"That's the one. I have always loved dancing." Despite the coffee, I suppressed a yawn. I glanced down at my watch. It was already almost 11pm!

"I should probably get going," I said. "Thank you for dinner and the coffee. I had a wonderful time."

"Okay, thank you. It has been great to get to know you, Miss Tanna. Would you mind if I walked you home? I wouldn't want any thugs to kidnap you on this fine evening."

"Of course. I wouldn't want that either," I grinned.

As we walked to my villa, Tony held my hand. I squeezed it back in rapture. He was holding my hand! I looked at our fingers and thought two hands never fit so well together. He paused as we reached my door. I wondered if he was going to kiss me, but he leaned in, brushed his cheek lightly against mine in a European-style farewell that sent waves of shock through my system, and said thank you for a wonderful evening. All I could do was nod. He said good night and walked back to his villa.

With shaking hands, I tried to open my door. It took a couple tries, but I eventually got in. I went into the bathroom, alight with butterflies and anticipation. I wondered if I'd ever be able to fall asleep tonight. I took off my makeup, washed my face, and changed into my cozy pajamas. As I climbed into the crisp white sheets, my head swirled with the events of the last couple of days. I had not only found a jewel in the ocean, but I had just spent the evening with a jewel of a man. I could definitely feel myself falling for this Adonis. As I went to bed, I hoped I would dream of coffee creamer, lobster dinners, and one particularly tall man.

Chapter 9

My dream was so real. It wasn't a pleasant Maldives' experience; no cute dark-haired men were in it. I started on a bus ride taking a group of people to the city. The bus was traveling mostly downhill, but it jerked twice, and we lurched forward. Hearing the sputtering noise, I knew it couldn't be good. The bus driver eased the bus to the side of the road. He waited, then turned the key in the ignition. Nothing. He tried it again, but still nothing. He waited and tried again. In my mind, I was already making plans what to do.

It was January and freezing cold. Everyone put their coats on and piled out of the bus. At this point, the driver was on his cell phone calling the bus station for help. After finishing his conversation, he informed us that help was on the way and another bus would arrive, but he didn't give us a specific time when it would show up. We had a choice, wait in the bus or walk down into the valley.

I decided to brave it on my own. I had a knitted hat, warm black boots reaching to my knees, gloves, and a parka that hugged me like three soft fuzzy blankets. Snow was all around. I was definitely not in the Maldives anymore. Some people climbed back on the bus. Instead of taking the road that the bus was on, I decided to take a shortcut which would lead to the city, but I would get there quicker. I knew it was only a mile or two.

I started walking in the direction of the familiar city lights. As I started my journey, I felt confident. After I had walked about a quarter of a mile, I found myself at a crossroads. The path had led me to a lake. I looked to the left and noticed big boulders that looked impossible to pass. The right side of the lakeshore met with a mountain wall which looked to be an opening of a cave. I had to make a choice. I could walk in the water and swim across. I knew that was ridiculous because I would surely freeze to death. I could do the large boulders and probably fall in the water or select the cave which was unknown and petrified me.

As I stood pondering my options with fear rising in my chest, a new fear approached from the opposite shore. Suddenly, I heard something coming out of the trees from across the way. A gorgeous tiger appeared bearing an impressive set of dangerous fangs. Suddenly the tiger jumped in the water with a splash and proceeded to swim straight toward me. My stomach clenched in fright. What was I going to do? Every option seemed blocked. The option of swimming in the water was out because I would freeze, and the tiger would eat my frozen body. The option of trying to stay upright while balancing on icy boulders was out because instinct told me I would probably end up in the frigid water.

My game of eenie, meeny, miny, mo was costing me precious time as the tiger was halfway across the lake now, but I felt frozen and couldn't move. Suddenly in a moment of decision, I ran faster than I have ever run in my life toward the cave. I was scared beyond words because of the unknown inhabitants of the cave, but the thought of the approaching tiger drove me on. I did not look back. Inside the cave was very dark, but as I ran, my eyes started to adjust.

As I crept my way farther into the tunnel, it got darker and darker until the light was completely gone. I had to slow my pace and inch my way along by feeling the side of the cave wall. The rock was cold and wet. I stumbled along for a while when I noticed a faint light appear at the end of the tunnel. The light grew larger as I moved forward. I felt relief sweep through me.

Eventually, I saw a wide opening and light burst through. It was the sun and as I picked up my pace and ran a few more feet, and I was out of the cave. I kept on running until I saw a tree, a small emblem of hope that I could hide behind. Tears streamed down my cheeks as I threw my arms around the tree and hugged it. Only then was I brave enough to peek back at the tunnel.

I didn't hear any loud growling, heavy tiger breathing, or his footsteps coming after me. It was like he had dissipated like a wisp of smoke. I continued to stand behind my safety tree. At that point, I wondered at the spirit that had carried me through the labyrinth of fear and uncertainty. I spotted the path and got back on it, glancing back once again. I walked fast and sometimes I jogged. When the first city lights appeared, I cried hard. I realized that my quick thinking and unyielding bravery had brought me to this point of safety.

I woke up the same way. I pulled the soft sheet and blanket up to my neck. I cried hot bitter tears, reached for the Kleenex box, and cried again. It had felt so real.

It didn't take long for me to start put meaning to the dream. It felt like a metaphor for everything I had been feeling lately. The dream reminded me of my own life because I was scared to venture out, be brave, and change courses. I did feel a satisfying sense of pride that I had taken the unknown path and escaped the tiger. I had shown bravery. I continued to cry because even though I was sad, I also felt free that I had moved out of limbo to newer ground and more elevated heights.

I wished I was in Tony's arms. I wished he was able to read my mind and would knock on my door and take me in his arms without asking me a single question. If he saw the look on my face, he would know. Once again, I was struck with a feeling that I had met him or known him from somewhere else, and that I had felt his tender kindness before. But where or when? It was draining my already low energy to try and figure it out. I could see a wet spot on my pillow from my tears.

I lay back down and tried to get some more sleep.

Chapter 10

When I woke up the next morning, I kept thinking about the dream from last night. While in the shower, my thoughts moved to the third Indiana Jones movie. In order for Indy to save his father, he needed to take the leap of faith, which meant walking through dangerous places to find the Holy Grail, fill it with holy water, and bring it back to heal his father who had been shot. My mind wandered to the most remarkable scene, where Indy is required to somehow move from one cliff to another with no path in sight. When he takes a deep breath, closes his eyes, and takes a step off the cliff, miraculously, the path is shown to him, and the way forward becomes visible. It was with that leap of faith that the camera moves to the side of him, and the clear path becomes visible.

I received a notification on my phone. It was a message from my sister, Cassandra, who was supposed to be joining me the next day. The text message read: *Tanna, I'm so sorry I can't come to join you. Annabelle [her daughter] was in a car accident. The doctors think she will be okay, but I can't leave her. I know you will have a great time and meet some fun people. Have fun. I can't wait to hear all about it. Love Cassandra.*

I texted her back and wished Sabrina all the best and my love. Then the dreaded thought came to me that I would be spending the rest of the Christmas vacation alone. My mind raced to all the holidays I'd be spending on my own from now on, and the thought depressed me. But, then I remembered Tony. He had come out of no where and had been such excellent company during this vacation. Maybe divorce didn't need to mean the end of my social life. Even if I was living on my own and vacationing on my own, maybe it didn't have to be lonely. Maybe I could handle it, and especially if Tony were there, maybe I wouldn't be alone for Christmas after all.

Don't get ahead of yourself, Tanna. I thought. *One step at a time*, I reminded myself. I could handle breakfast. I had done it before. I got up, made myself presentable, placed my jewel securely in an inner pocket of my bag, and went to the food court.

I played the same game of standing at my table looking around, pretending to survey the situation, but in actuality, I was looking for Tony. Unfortunately, I didn't see him. So, I ate a quiet breakfast of quesadillas filled with ham, scrambled egg, green onions, cilantro, and green salsa with a lightly toasted flour tortilla. Avocado toast caught my eye with bright green smashed fruit, sprinkled with "everything but the bagel" sesame seasoning. I also grabbed coffee and juice. As I was returning my tray, someone tapped me on the arm from behind. I turned around to see Abbey with a miniature cinnamon roll in one hand and her yellow string in the other.

"Hi Tanna! Can you teach me the other tricks?"

I had made a date with myself to go to town and check out the jewelers shop and see if I could get any intel on my gemstone. I told her I couldn't right now, but I would be back in the afternoon and would show her. She seemed pleased and ran back to family. I heard her explain to them that I would help her later in a voice for all the food court guests to hear.

I was excited to find out the origin of my gemstone and see what I could do with it. I spent a little time texting my sister to get an update on her daughter before I walked out without my wide-brimmed hat, turned around, walked right back in to grab my hat, and headed toward town. The jewel was safely in my bag.

I headed straight for the "Best Jewelry Shop in the Maldives," that I had seen when I came to the city earlier. The jeweler was behind the counter, so I walked over to him. He smiled and asked if he could help me. His name-tag said his name was Ibrahim.

"Good morning," I said as I reached into my bag to pull out the gemstone. "I have something I'd like you to take a look at. Perhaps you can tell me a little more about it."

I brought out the jewel which I had wrapped in tissue and held it in my hand. The jeweler reached under the counter and brought out a folded rectangle of black velvet, which he unfolded and placed on the counter. I sat the jewel on the display cloth and moved my head as the light in the room caught several facets of the stone.

"Where did you get this?" He asked as he reached under the cabinet again and pulled out a magnifier to study it more closely.

"I found it in the ocean. I wanted to have you inspect it to see what it is, or even have some jewelry made from it. And maybe you can help me determine where it came from. It doesn't seem like the type of rock you would typically find in the ocean."

He turned the gemstone over and examined it with his special-ized eyepiece before setting the jewel back on the glass surface again. He looked at me. "So you found it around here?"

"Yeah, when I was snorkeling."

"That's not something you see every day in these parts. If I'm correct, this jewel comes from pegmatite, which are igneous rocks composed of interlocking crystals. They're actually not found around here. They are found in Brazil and Madagascar. It looks like Madagascan rose quartz. It is of fine quality and in high demand." I imagined myself wearing pretty bright pink stud earrings with a matching teardrop necklace.

"Wow, so what was it doing in the ocean here?"

"I have a theory about that. I've been reading some articles online of some underhanded trading between Madagascar and the Maldives. The trading vessels have been avoiding custom tax laws and trading jewels like this illicitly. I'm pretty sure this was probably brought from Madagascar to the Maldives on one of those ships. We have ships sailing from other countries importing almost everything. It's pretty easy for them to sneak around the law enforcement. They know what they are doing. If this one was lost from the original loot, I'm sure a jewel of this size would be noticed missing. The people who stole it will probably come back to recover it. I can't be certain, of course, but this gemstone fits the description of some of the articles I've read of the kind of contraband these criminals are trading on the black market."

The wooden door to the jewelry shop opened, but I didn't pay much attention as I was too enraptured with the jeweler's story. Suddenly, the jeweler moved the jewel into my hand, folded up the black piece of velvet, and stuffed it behind it behind his counter. He stared into my eyes as if to say, *Hide the jewel quickly.* I pulled my bag to my front and dropped it in with no one noticing. It would have appeared to anyone who walked in the store that we had just been talking.

I turned around as the door slammed shut and saw three men whom I suspected were Maldivian. They were about the same height as the jewelry store owner and all three had black hair. They walked to the front of the display case.

I moved aside. I saw their angry faces and stepped closer to the wall to give them their space. They yelled at the jeweler in an accusing tone. Although I didn't know what they were saying because they were speaking in Dhivehi, I knew it was not a peaceful conversation. The man on the left yelled at the jeweler. The second man pointed to me. I saw the jeweler shrug his shoulders and raise his hands to show his palms and start to back away.

The man in the middle glanced at me every few seconds while his partner yelled at the jeweler. He kept looking at my bag, which I kept clutched to my front.

Oh no, they are going to grab my bag and steal my gemstone, I thought. I eased farther away. The man in the middle turned toward me and took a step looking threatening.

At that moment, the door bells chimed, and to my intense relief, Tony walked in. I have never been so happy to see him in all my life. He walked into the store with authority. I ran to him, and he put his arm around me. I was safe. The three men stood for another few seconds and realized their visit was futile after shouting threats to the jeweler. They shook their fists at the jeweler and then at me. *What had I done? Why would they shake their fists at me?* The men made a point to slam the door on their way out.

"Tony, how did you know?" I blurted out.

"I didn't know. I was having some ice cream down the boardwalk when I saw you come into the store. I saw those men go in after you a while later, and I didn't like the look on their faces when they went in. When I didn't see you come out immediately, I thought I would come to check things out. I know you're a grown woman and can handle yourself on your own, but it doesn't hurt to have some backup now and again."

I reached up and kissed him on the cheek. I couldn't help myself. I had been so scared. I could see he was pleasantly surprised and might have kissed me back if we were alone. Then I remembered the jeweler.

"Oh, this is my friend Tony," I said to Ibrahim. "We are staying in the bungalows." I pointed in that direction of the resort. Tony bowed his head in acknowledgment.

Ibrahim nodded to Tony. He put his hand to his lips as though he wanted us to stop talking. He walked over to the door, flipped the sign to closed, and locked the door with a silver skeleton key. Then he went over and pulled down the tan-colored shades before turning to Tony.

"Does he know about what you found?" I said that he did. "Is it okay if I tell him what I told you?" I nodded.

The jeweler told Tony what he told me about the gemstone. He said he suspected these were common pirate thieves who were working on the black market. He suspected they were looking for the beautiful pink stone I had. Somehow, they suspected I it. Why they thought I had the jewel, he didn't know. I had no idea how I had tipped them off. The only thing I could imagine was if they had somehow seen me with the stone when I was snorkeling. I thought back to my snorkeling adventure and could not remember anyone watching me.

The jeweler asked if I would like him to hold onto the gemstone until I decided what to do with it. I thought for a moment and told him I would take it with me. I wanted to report it to security.

Tony said in a decent James Arness impression pretending to tip a cowboy hat, "Well, little lady, what do you say we grab the loot, round up our horses and get out of Dodge as fast as humanly possible?"

I laughed. I loved the TV series *Gunsmoke*. The jeweler smiled, too. Tony always had a way of making me laugh and letting me know that things are not quite as bad as I envisioned them to be.

Ibrahim suggested that we go out the back way. He led us to the wooden stairs. The stairs had chipped and were peeling paint so I didn't slide my hand along the banister to avoid slivers. I held on tight to my bag. When we reached a room at the top, there was more light streaming in the windows, and I could see all sorts of jewelry-making equipment and several piles of unpolished rocks.

The jeweler pointed to another set of stairs. We thanked him, said goodbye, and headed that direction. We found our way to the outside of the building. It was an alley, so we quickly headed for the main street. When we turned the corner and sneaked a glance at the jewelry shop, the shades were up so the sun streamed in. The sign was flipped to
"Open" again. We walked quickly away. We could see Ibrahim back at his place behind the counter.

I told Tony I would like to buy him a smoothie to thank him for his gallantry. He said it was unnecessary but agreed to it anyway.

Since I had already been to one coffee shop in the Maldives city, I suggested we go to a different one. Tony hadn't been to any of the coffee shops in the Maldives yet, so he followed my lead. Walking into the Café Maldives, I breathed deeply, taking in the scent of freshly ground coffee. We ordered a couple of refreshing smoothies. It was too hot for coffee right now.

"Thanks again, Tony. I don't know what would have happened if you hadn't come into the jewelry shop at the right time. I was scared they were going to get physical, punch my lights out, and steal my bag. I didn't have a clue what they were saying. But I knew it wasn't in my favor."

"I think you handled it really well," he said.

"Thank you."

"What are you going to do with the jewel?" he asked.

"I think I will take it to the hotel and ask for security and see what they say. I'll explain the situation. Maybe they will have some advice. Do you think those guys will try to bother me again? They probably know where I am staying."

"Well, as you know I am close by. I can get there pretty quick."

"You're a lifesaver. Thanks for offering."

We finished our drinks and walked out of the coffee shop. We didn't have much of a desire to shop, so we headed back to our bungalows. I wanted to lay in my pool with my eyes closed. Tony said that he would try to come by a little later. I hoped he would pop over and join me in my pool. He said he had some work to do though, so we parted.

I headed to the security office where I could take my pink stone. In my heart of hearts, I wanted to keep it. I could take it back to the States with me. I could have earrings and a necklace made from it. It was like I had found a treasure.

I did my best to talk myself into keeping the gemstone.

No one would ever know, right? Except I would. And I guess Tony would too.

After staring at the ocean for what seemed like an eternity and weighing my choices, I turned and walked into the main court and asked for a security guard. He ushered me into his office. I sat down but didn't talk for a moment.

After gathering my courage, I said, "I found something in the ocean. I think it might have been stolen and dropped off in the water to avoid detection. I took it to a jeweler, and he said that the jewel was from Madagascar. Also, it is possible some people have been hunting me down trying to get it back. Somehow, they must have seen me take it from the ocean. I felt I should return it, anyway. So here it is."

I reached into my bag and brought out the jewel. It was so beautiful, I once again questioned my decision to turn it in, but I knew I needed to do the right thing and report it. I placed the stone on the desk in front of the officer.

He picked up the jewel, rubbed it with his fingers, and brought it closer to his eyes. "That's a beauty," he said. "We haven't had any reports of anything gone missing. I don't see how we could prove this was contraband, if it was. I think you can keep it." He handed it back to me.

"Thank you for your help." Wow! I got to keep it! I couldn't wait to tell Tony. I wanted to take the jewel back to town and have Ibrahim make it into some earrings and a necklace for me.

Back in my bungalow, I wiggled into my two-piece swimsuit, grabbed a towel, a coverlet, my hat, the sunscreen, and I was out the door. I slathered on the broad-spectrum SPF 70. That should keep the sun in its place and away from my tender skin for a while.

I closed my eyes and let the perfect temperature water work its magic over my body and mind.

All I could hear were muffled sounds of people walking and talking on the boardwalk, like when I was snorkeling underwater. My mind wandered back in time to when I was a little girl. Even though I was young and have forgotten some of the details of this particular memory, I cherished what I could remember.

Chapter 11

It had been a hot day. I remember the crunching sound of the car as it travelled up the dirt road to the pavilion for our family reunion. A cloud of dust followed us. We walked from our car to the shade of the pavilion and placed a covered dish on the serving table. Others did the same. You could smell those home-baked dishes right when you stepped out of your car. We had traveled all the way from California to Alabama for this reunion of my mom's family. It was her favorite day of the year. There was golden fried chicken, cornbread with butter and honey, hummingbird cake, and fried okra. I could almost smell them as I lay in the water with my head on the side of the pool.

The rule at the reunion, which my mother had made up on the spot to get us to eat, was that we had to finish our food before playing. All I could see was the playground with swings, slides, teeter-totters, and monkey bars a few feet away from me. I ate as fast as I could while all the older folks ate slowly, talking and laughing as though time really didn't exist. When I finished my food, I ran to the merry-go-round first.

A boy was holding on tight and running to make it go faster, then he would jump on and enjoy the ride. When he saw me, he let it slow down, and I jumped on. I kicked my flip-flops off and watched them fly through the air and hit the ground as I flew past. The boy, I think his name was Dean, something like that, jumped off and pushed hard to move it faster. I sat on the ride holding on tight with both hands, the breeze flying through my hair.

We played all afternoon, while the adults sat in the pavilion fanning their faces. My new friend and I laughed as he pushed my swing, then ran underneath me. We sat in the sand and dug our toes down deep and buried them.

While we were watching our toes burrow deep in the sand then pop up, a blonde bully came up from behind me and dumped a plastic bucket of sand on my head. The sand was hot; the air was muggy, and I felt deflated. I sat there with sand falling off my head with my tears joining it.

My friend said there was a water faucet where I could wash off. He pointed where it was.

"Everything will be okay. I'll be right back." Dean jumped up and ran after the kid. The kid ran fast laughing and looking back to see if he could outrun Dean. Dean was faster. He caught up with him, grabbed him around the chest, and tackled him to the ground. Dean grabbed his arm and forced it behind his back, as though he would handcuff him.

"Why did you do that?" Dean yelled at him and waited for an answer. I could still hear them from where I was in the sandbox.

When the kid didn't answer, Dean pulled his arms tighter around his back.

The kid yelled. "Okay, okay. I had this bucket of sand, and I thought it would be funny to pour it on her head, and I thought she would think it was funny."

Dean glared at him. "Now do you think it's funny?" pinning the bully to the ground.

"No," the bully frowned.

"Alright now listen. You owe someone an apology. We are going to go back, and you will do the talking."

"Okay, okay. I will."

Dean let him up but watched him so he wouldn't run away. The kid trudged back to where I was still shaking my head and brushing the sticky sand off my arms and face.

The kid was slow to speak but finally said, "I'm sorry." He looked at Dean. Dean nodded. The kid turned around and ran off. I was glad to see him go. Dean extended his hand to me and pulled me up so we could walk over to the water faucet. The water felt cool on my hot sandy skin. I cupped my hands together, gathered the water, and splashed it on my face over and over. My clothes were getting wet, but I didn't care. I bathed my arms and legs with cool water.

Finally, I laughed, bent down, and put my head directly under the faucet. I rubbed the sand out of my hair, and Dean rubbed my arms and shoulders with the cool water. Dean said there was a towel in his car in case they went swimming. He ran for the towel, and I stayed by the faucet. I finished rinsing all the sand out of my hair.

I towel dried my hair, and after I dried the rest of myself off, I wrapped the towel around my shoulders. We sat on the two vacant swings, pushing ourselves slowly with our feet. I purposely stayed in rhythm with him.

For some reason, I remembered the moment while I sat in the cool refreshing pool. I remembered how I felt and how I didn't want it to end. That boy was my rescuer and in a matter of a few hours, he became my best friend. I was only a little girl, but there was a peaceful calm that I had met someone really special.

Dean turned to me. "Will you be here next year?" I told him I didn't know. Dean said he and his family were visiting his grandparents nearby. He wasn't there as part of the family reunion. He didn't know when they would come to visit again.

But then I saw my mom motion for me to come. It was time to go. I did what any little girl who had just found a best friend would do—I ignored her. About two minutes later, she caught my attention and called my name with that *get over here* look on her face, and I knew I better not to ignore her this time.

I stood up, touched his arm, and he grabbed my hand like he didn't want to let it go.

"Bye Dean."

"Bye."

I pulled away and walked to our car but turned to watch Dean with every few steps. Dean's feet were on the ground slowly pushing himself back and forth in the swing. He never took his eyes off me. When I opened the car door to get in, I closed the door but stared back at Dean through the window. My dad looked in the backseat to make sure everyone was accounted for, started the car, and we left in a cloud of dust, just like when we had arrived.

After that year, our family missed the reunion for a few years for different reasons, and then when we did go, Dean wasn't there. I never saw him again. One year while I was sitting on the swing without Dean, I vowed I wanted to marry him. If I couldn't marry him, then I wanted to marry someone just like him.

I never found out his last name. We were just kids, and it didn't seem important to gather personal details like last names. I think we assumed that we would meet up again the next year but never did.

I opened my eyes. My eyes took a few seconds to adjust to the bright sun. Had I dozed off and my memory became a dream? As everything came into view, I smiled thinking about my memories. No one could be that great. Not Dean, not anyone.

I heard some footsteps behind me. A pair of warm hands covered my eyes softly, "Guess who?"

"Take a seat, Tony."

"How'd you know it was me?" he asked sounding surprised.

"I could tell you didn't have the hands of a nine-year-old girl. And you and she are really the only ones I know here."

He kicked off his flip-flops. He walked into the water, sat down and shared the step with me. "Anything new?"

"You know my sister that was going to meet me here and stay in the extra room in my villa? Well, she won't be coming now," I said.

"How come?"

"Her daughter was in a car accident."

His eyes widened. "Oh, I'm so sorry. Is she okay?"

"Her daughter will be okay. She's in the hospital, but it's not life-threatening. But my sister didn't want to leave and be halfway around the world."

I thought for a moment about what Cassandra had said about meeting more outgoing people and then asked Tony, "Am I outgoing enough for you, Tony?"

He thought for a moment and said with a sly smile, "Actually, Tanna, you were a little aggressive when we first met. Maybe tone it down a little." My heart sank. He laughed. "I'm kidding, you were just right. In fact, if you had been too aggressive, that would have turned me off, and I would have looked for less aggressive fish in less aggressive waters."

What was it about this man? I wished he would quit saying the perfect things in response to what I said, because it was making it easier and easier to fall for him.

"So, tell me more about yourself," I said, changing the subject.

He raised an eyebrow. "Does this have anything to do with you wanting to know my middle name?"

I laughed. "Well yeah, of course I want to know your middle name, but I also want to know what makes you tick."

"What makes me tick is, I suppose, my heart."

"Okay, but when I am around you, I feel something."

"Is that something bad or good?" he asked.

"It's good, or I wouldn't have let you into my pool, and we wouldn't be talking. Tony, are you sure we have never met before? I get this weird feeling of déjà vu when I am with you."

He thought for a moment. "You already asked me that, and I don't see how we could have. You live in that beautiful state of California, and I have never lived outside of the South. Born and raised. Do I remind you of someone you know?" Tony asked after a pause.

"I have tried to think of where I could have possibly met you but cannot. Maybe you do remind me of someone. Could we have met on another planet, in a different dimension?" I teased half seriously. "Did we know each other in a different life?"

"I hope so," he smiled. "That would make a pretty great story. I can see the headlines now. 'Two lovers from a former life find each other.'" Although Tony seemed to think it was funny, I was still racking my brain as to why he seemed so familiar.

But it remained an enigma. Did I have to know the answer to be with him? Did I have to know the answer to continue living my life and be happy?

I looked at the man beside me. Whoever he was or where he came from didn't matter. He was here. I was here. We were in one of the most beautiful places on planet Earth, and that was enough for now.

My stomach growled, reminding me it had been a while since I'd eaten. All I had for lunch was that smoothie.

Tony must have read my mind. "How about we go to dinner?"

"Sure," I said.

We got out of the pool and said we'd meet in a half an hour. I got dressed in record time met him on the main boardwalk. Tony looked at me intently. His eyes were piercingly blue. He seemed to have something on his mind. I looked down at my dress feeling suddenly self-conscious.

"Penny for your thoughts?" I broke the silence.

"I was just thinking about kissing you," he said. Oh, phew! I was glad that we were on the same page about that. But like my mother taught me, I tried to play coy.

"Listen honey, if you play your cards right, you never know what'll happen," I said. He held my hand, and we walked like junior high kids swinging our arms as walked toward the food court.

At dinner I sat across from Tony. "So Tanna, have you figured out my middle name yet?" he asked. I had a feeling he would bring this up, and I had a few guesses.

"Maybe."

"Okay, shoot."

"Sheldon?"

"Nope. Try again."

"Okay, it starts with an S right?" He nodded. "Okay, Simon?" He shook his head. I started listing off every S name I could think of: "Sterling, Spencer, Sean, Stetson, Seth, Sebastian?"

He laughed. "You have been giving this some thought. It's not any of those. Remember, it's seven letters. It's not going to be as easy as that. I would be surprised if you came up with it. It's an old family name."

"So, how about another clue?"

"Sure, let me think. Okay, the next clue is, it ends with an N."

"Really, N? I thought it would narrow it down." I paused a second, counted letters on my finger, "Is it Stephen?" I hoped. "Sampson?"

"Good guesses, but no."

"Okay, I'm down for the count. I will have to keep thinking. Are you sure this is a real name?"

"Well it's mine, so it's got to be."

"What will you give me if I guess it right?"

"Oh, I'm sure we could come up with a fair exchange," he winked, which sent a thrill down my legs. Gosh this man was beautiful. How was this real? How was I on a second date with this man?

We went to some lounge chairs and watched the final moments of the sunset and continued talking. I never thought I could talk to someone so easily. I was out of the dating game for so long. I thought this would be so much harder, but talking to Tony was like talking to an old friend, only we had a lot more ground to cover.

It was starting to get dark. I asked Tony if he was going to the Fire and Light Show on the mainland. He said he had to work and hoped I would enjoy it. I wondered what could be so important as to miss it. But I suppose work came first.

Tony walked me to my door, stood for a moment, bent his head toward mine, and kissed me gently on the lips, which sent a zing through me. It left me wishing for a longer kiss.

"To be continued," he said. I couldn't wait. "Can I see you again tomorrow night?"

I got ready for bed and finished the evening catching the end of one of my favorite movies on TV; *Gone With the Wind* was on. Oh that Rhett Butler. What a hunk. But for the first time when watching this movie, I didn't picture myself with Rhett Butler. Instead, I fantasized about being with another dashing southern gentleman.

Chapter 12

The next day, I spent the majority of the day lounging at the beach. I wanted to work on my tan. I read *The Awakening* under an umbrella. I watched a bunch of local children playing with bowls and spoons in the sand. I had seen tons of beach toys in one of the shops while I was shopping for my Christmas gifts for my grandchildren. I thought that tomorrow I would go back and get some and bring them to the beach for any kids that wanted to play. I thought maybe Abbey and her sister might want some too.

As I read my book and fell into the story with Edna Pontellier, I missed Tony. He never made me feel the way Edna's husband made her feel. Unappreciated, ornamental. However, that was often how I felt with Jeff. Maybe that was one reason I loved this book so much. I related to Edna on so many levels. Although I had no intention of ending my story the way she ended hers. I couldn't wait to see Tony again. He reinvigorated my belief in love and *joie de vivre*. He had sent a note to my room asking if he could see me again. He said he would need to spend the day working, but if he had time, he would try to meet me at the fire show that night.

So when the time came, I walked across the boardwalk to where the show would start. The show started with pacific islander attire.

The men wore ivory tooth necklaces, bare feet, and a simple yellow cloth headband with fabric covering from the waist to the knee. Their short fabric skirts were tan with long grass leggings that reached from the lower knee to the ankle. Bare chests probably made it easier to throw fire sticks around so their clothing didn't catch on fire.

The lights went out after I found a place to sit at the back. Everyone in the audience sat in awe of the man on stage who waved his fire stick, lit on both ends like a baton in a marching band. He even brought the stick to his mouth so the fire touched his lips. It looked like the fire stayed on his lips for two seconds. Then he laid down and placed the fire stick on both feet for five seconds.

We all screamed in excitement and horror. He jumped up as we breathed a loud sigh of relief. The adrenaline in the place was palpable. If that wasn't enough to make us crazy, seven more men with fire sticks came out and performed together, all swinging their sticks so fast, it looked like giant sparklers on the Fourth of July.

Six ladies entered from both sides of the back of the stage, three on one side and three on the other, and wore fresh-cut flower crowns in their hair. Their clothes were sky blue fabric with no sleeves and stopped just above the knee. They clapped and sang. Their performance was much less dramatic than the fire stick event, meaning I could breathe a little easier.

At intermission, I played my same sneaky trick of standing up to appear like I was stretching, all the while scanning the audience in the hopes that Tony had come to the show even though he said he would be working.

Miracle of miracles, I spotted him, and my heart skipped a beat. I watched him search the crowd, maybe for a seat, but I hoped he was searching for me. He raised his eyebrows and grinned when his eyes landed on me. He motioned for me to come down to where he was and pointed to two vacant seats. I walked past all the knees and feet and tried not to tromp on them, making my way to him. I kept my eye on Tony as I walked.

"Is this seat taken?" I asked him, smiling.

"Yes, I'm waiting for someone. You." My heart thudded in my chest and my face flushed. I hoped he couldn't see. Luckily Abbey came around the corner.

"Tanna! Tanna!" I turned my face away from Tony's gaze and waved to Abbey and her family.

I slipped in beside Tony, and we continued to stand during the last part of intermission.

"How did work go today?"

"It went well. I just wish I didn't have to work while on vacation, but some things can't be helped. Besides, it took a whole day of time I could have been spending with my favorite lady." I blushed. "How has the show been?"

"It's been excellent so far. You are in for a real treat. It doesn't get any better unless you go straight to Hawaii and take in the Polynesian Cultural Center show, and the luau is fabulous."

"I've never been, but I have heard it's great."

The second half of the show started with a little more of the same and a few different songs and dances. We cheered and clapped for the dancers and singers who bowed and pounded on their chests, while the women singers blew kisses to us.

As the show ended and the house lights came up, the guests filed past us, but we stayed in our seats to let everyone pass.

Tony asked if I would like to stop by the bar and get a beer. I didn't answer. I wanted to say yes, but I wasn't a drinker. If I turned him down, would he leave? But I decided honesty was the best policy.

"I, um, I'm not much of a drinker."

To my surprise, his face lit up. "Neither am I. I was just checking because I didn't want to go to a bar only for you to drink and get plastered, and I'd have to mop you up off the floor."

We both laughed.

"How about a Coke?" he suggested.

"Cherry, please," I said.

The bar was filled with so much noise when we walked through the door that I couldn't hear Tony's words about where to sit. After I said "what?" twice, he gave up and pointed to a table for two. I lead the way. I didn't usually go to bars, but tonight it seemed appropriate after the delightful show presented by the local men and women from the Maldives. I felt like a little celebration was in order.

"How'd you like the show?" I asked Tony. I realized I had to practically shout for all the barroom noise, so I leaned my head toward him to ask.

"Well, I only saw the second half, but I thought it was great."

"Yeah, me too. I really liked the men throwing fire sticks and spinning them like batons. That had us all on pins and needles. But thankfully none of the men caught on fire."

We made small chat for a while until we got to the subject of dreams. I told him about my dream with the tiger and the cave.

He seemed impressed. "I don't often remember my dreams as vividly as that," he said. "Except for last night actually." He looked thoughtful as if wondering what to say next. He looked at me closely and said, "Can I tell you about it?"

I had the feeling he was going to share something special, and I got goosebumps. I said, "Tell me."

We were still speaking louder than usual, so I moved closer and strained my ears so I could hear Tony's dream. With Tony's elbows on the table and his fingers intertwining and touching his chin, he spoke about his dream.

He started, "Ok, in my dream, I was at my home looking out the window. Two stars caught my attention. They were on opposite sides of the horizon. They seemed to be the brightest stars in the sky. All the others twinkled and were very beautiful, but these two stars outshone them all. I turned away from the window to watch my kids playing games."

Tony paused to clarify, "My children were younger in my dream than they are now."

"Ok," I said and he went on.

"The children took a break and walked out of the room. I stood up and looked out the window again. Both stars had moved in an upward direction in a straight line, moving straight up into the sky. They were no longer on the horizon. They moved quickly. I got distracted helping my kids get ready for bed. As I was urging them to get up and go brush their teeth, my gaze drifted to the window again. The stars had definitely moved again farther upward in the sky, this time upward but starting a curving motion toward each other to form a half circle." He indicated the movement with this fingers.

"I stood still and watched the two stars, looking from one to the other. I had the distinct impression they were headed toward each other. All of a sudden, they stopped. Neither star moved for the rest of my dream. I would turn away, then check back and their positions in the nighttime sky wouldn't change. Tanna, I can't describe the feeling. I can't think of a better word to describe it than 'magic.' It was as if time stood still, and the universe was aware of me watching the two stars. It felt important. It reminds me of an idea I once read about online called the Quantum Observer Effect. Have you ever heard of it?"

I shook my head.

"It's something in quantum physics. I don't understand it fully; however, physicists found that research suggests that a conscious mind can directly affect reality. So observing something can change the results. You with me so far?" I nodded.

"You know when you wake up from a dream, and it feels so real? It feels more like a memory. The essence of it all stays with you. This dream was like that for me. It was hard to shake it for a while. It has affected the way I see what's around me, affecting my reality."

Tony stopped talking and closed his eyes. I could only imagine he was feeling that magic of his dream right now. He opened his eyes and looked at me, "I know this sounds strange, and I don't know why I'm telling you, except it made a big impression on me, and I feel comfortable telling you. I hope it wasn't inappropriate." He shrugged his shoulders. "After all, we've only known each other a few days."

"True." I answered.

He continued. "It almost felt like my destiny, like I was one of those stars heading for home. Like I was getting closer to where I was supposed to be the closer I got to the other star. Does that make any sense?"

"Yeah it does. That's a beautiful idea, two stars at home with each other. That's pretty special. Thanks for telling me."

"What do you think it meant when the two stars started to move toward each other like magnets? And why did they stop? I guess they stopped because I was watching them, but what would happen if they finally met up?"

"I don't know. Do you think dreams help us express our innermost thoughts or maybe tell our future?" I asked.

"Maybe." Tony looked at his watch and said, "I've been talking for a long time. Let's talk about you. What else can you tell me about yourself, Tanna?"

"Do you want to guess my middle name?"

He laughed. "Sure!" He shifted in his seat to a more relaxed position.

"Okay, Tony, I will give you clues, and you will probably guess it in under two minutes. Unlike your most uncommon middle name, my middle name is relatively common. Your first clue is that it is the name of a Disney princess."

"I don't know all the Disney princesses, I'm afraid," he paused for a second. "Is it Ariel?"

"Nope. Try again."

"Hmm, let me think. Cinderella?"

I laughed. "Have you ever met a Cinderella?"

"No, but I don't remember the princesses much. Can I have another hint?"

"It starts with B."

"Oh that narrows it down. B. ... Bambi, no that's not my guess, hold on. It isn't that gal from Beauty and the Beast, is it? Give me a second, it will come to me. ... Barbara, Betty, no." He looked up after a moment. "Is it Belle?"

"Yes, it is. Well done."

"That's pretty. Tanna Belle," he repeated. It sounded so beautiful when he said it. "Why did your parents choose Belle?"

"Well, I'm named after my grandmother, Minnie Belle. To continue the tradition, my kids gave Belle as a middle name to two of their children. Incidentally, my mom's side of the family is from the South, like I said, so maybe that helped inspire the name initially."

"It's a beautiful name."

"Thank you. I've always liked it."

One subject led to another and whether I liked it or not, we eventually started talking about our exes. I suppose it was bound to happen eventually. We ordered another round.

"So why did you get divorced, if you don't mind me asking?" he said. "I want to understand why someone as wonderful as you is so conveniently single."

I let out a long sigh. "There's a short version and a long version. Which one do you want?"

"We have time. I'd like to hear both, if you don't mind," he said.

"Well, the short version is he cheated on me. But that oversimplifies things. That didn't end up being the reason I wanted a divorce. It was the nail in the coffin, but it wasn't like we had a great marriage to start with, and I think even if he hadn't cheated on me, we would have split up eventually.

"That definitely isn't how I thought it would be when I first got married. I was committed to making it work. I held on to a stigma against divorce. I didn't want to be one of those people that I thought 'gave up' on marriage. I always thought I would be different than that. I thought my marriage would be forever." I said. We sat in silence for a moment as I collected my thoughts.

"And for a long time, it wasn't all bad. I loved Jeff—or the part of Jeff that I chose to see. It took me a long time to admit that what I wanted to see wasn't the whole picture. He had the ability to shift from being completely charming and affectionate one minute (especially with other people around) to very distant, cold, and even cruel the next.

"The first part of our marriage was okay. Then as time went on, it got to be more bad times than good. There was no real change—except that he became more distant, more evasive, and less willing to communicate."

I looked around trying to make sense of it all. "You see, he liked to escape to his mother's house. He would spend days there at a time, especially after a fight. She'd cook his meals, do his laundry, and dote on him hand and foot, as she always had. And she never liked me much. I don't know why, but I guess that's the way with mothers and sons sometimes. She always seemed to push me away, once physically. She never liked the gifts I gave her for holidays or birthdays. I learned eventually if I bought something and made sure Jeff was the one to hand it to her, she would praise it and be completely thrilled.

"At home, I became more of a mother figure for him than anything else, I think. I think he lost the idea of me as a romantic partner and saw me as more of a roommate and housekeeper. And he would take his bad mood out on me. Not in physical violence but with sharp comments and dismissal. He put on this veneer of being independent and macho, but at home, he expected to be taken care of.

"The job of being his mother shouldn't have been mine, especially as I became a mother myself. Part of me always longed for that charming and debonair man I had met at the party when I was twenty, but after a while I realized I had played into his act. Sometimes I wonder if we would have stayed married very long if I hadn't gotten pregnant so quickly. At the time, I was completely besotted with him. I cherished the idea of a wonderful relationship where there was give and take, so willingly and so easily. Something like my parents had. And in the beginning, things were great. I wanted to be lovers together. I wanted to blend our minds as well as our bodies. But after our second daughter was in school, and he got more and more involved with his business schemes and his focus on his physique, he drifted away.

"I lived with the problems for a long time because I kept hoping it would repair itself and get better. Plus, when you have kids, life just kind of moves on without you having to give much thought to it. I was busy with them, and Jeff was busy with his stuff. And I figured every couple has problems, and people stay together. I remember thinking that a lot of people have it worse than I did, so I could suck it up and stay with my husband.

"When the thought of divorce finally entered my mind, it shocked me at first and felt really scary. I knew I didn't want to be a 'divorced person.' That wasn't me. And I saw what it did to my friend's family, and I never wanted to deal with that. The drama. I was trying so hard to keep a positive attitude. We were two different people, and because things started out so well when we were young and in love, I ignored our differences instead of seeing them for what they were."

I took a sip of my drink. Tony encouraged me to carry on. "We actually did go to a counselor for a few sessions. Things seemed to improve but only temporarily. I think being married presented problems that needed to be worked out, whereas going to his mother's, he was her little boy and back in safe territory. His mother should have kicked him out and said, 'Go home and eat with your wife,' but she prepared food for him like he was her tiny little boy again. Maybe it was a comfort to her too. I don't know."

I thought for a moment and went on. "When we married, I was trying to replicate Cinderella and 'live happily ever after.' And I thought that was how my marriage would be. No one talks about what happens after the marriage." I trailed off and stared at the wooden varnished table under my elbows.

I sat quietly and finally looked at Tony. He had a look of intense focus on his face. It gave me courage to continue.

"I have analyzed my situation to death. I have cut it into pieces, cross-sectioned it, and stared at all the pieces under a microscope repeatedly. I have looked at every aspect. In my efforts to be a good wife, I became a mother figure, which he wanted, but he also resented me for it. I thought it was love. Maybe it was at first. I don't know. I finally decided that two people who fall in love may not be the best for each other. Instead of bringing out the best in each other, the worst reared its ugly head. We were actually worse people when we were together."

I looked at him and saw he was still wearing that intense look on his face. "Tony do you follow me?" He was deep in thought. "Tanna to Tony. Tanna to Tony. Do you copy? Over."

He smiled. "I do get your drift about your marriage. So go on, what happened?"

"Well, I stayed in my marriage hoping for a miracle, but eventually he didn't want me anymore, and he chose someone else."

I waited for a moment to collect my thoughts and tell him about my resolution. "Since then, I have realized that if I want something to happen, I must get up and do something to make it happen. I was in a place where I could not progress. It's scary because fear ruled me. It stifled me. It stunted anything I might use to move forward. Fear of the unknown, fear because I wondered 'how did I get myself in this mess?' So I stayed because even though it was miserable, it was predictable and safe, and you don't have to venture into the unknown.

"When a person like me decides they have had enough, they choose to cut their losses and move on. But I cannot tell you how long it took. Once I decided to make that leap of faith and pursue my divorce, I felt better. Somehow, I didn't know how it would all work out, but I had the feeling it would be okay. So, handling the unknown led to something better than I hoped and dreamed for. It's how I ended up taking the leap of faith when I booked this trip that lead to me sitting here with you."

I felt like crying. I had told it all. I kept imagining the dream from last night as I was talking, and the truth of it hit me. A wave of emotion swept through me. My throat constricted, and I tried to swallow the lump that appeared in my throat. I sat quiet for a moment then brought both hands up to cover my face. I didn't want Tony to see me cry, but it looked like it was coming anyway. Even though I had only known him for four days, it felt like a lifetime. I wasn't crying because I was sad. I was crying because I felt a spark of joy and freedom from lifting a heaven burden.

There was still joy, happiness, and love in the world. I was feeling it now. Sitting with Tony gave me the calm I needed. I felt his hand on my arm handing me a napkin to catch the tears. I grabbed the napkin and hid my face behind the napkin. I didn't want to look at him with swollen and red eyes.

Tony stood up, walked to my side of the booth and sat down. He put his arm around me and pulled me close to him. Then his other arm circled around from the front of me and his fingers interlocked. It was the best bear hug I had ever received. Our heads were together. The next thing I knew, his lips were on my cheek with a gentle kiss. My tears slowed, and I pointed to the napkin holder for another. He immediately handed me two more through the opening in my hands.

When I could compose myself enough to talk, I said, "Tony, thank you for listening. What is your charge for a therapy session?" I asked as I dabbed my eyes.

We both chuckled a little, then sat in silence for a moment.

When I finally brought my hands away from my face, I stared straight forward. I finally got the courage to turn my head and look at him.

"Do I look like I've been crying?"

"Let me see." He reached under my chin and tilted my face towards his. "No, no evidence of tears, only your blue eyes sparkle so beautifully now."

He always said the best things. I smiled at his sweet comment.

We headed back to our bungalows. He led me to his door. "Would you like to come in?" he asked. "Yes, I think I can spare a few minutes," I agreed.

We walked onto his terrace and sat on the sofa chairs overlooking the moonlit ocean. He held my hand. He got up and turned on some music and came and sat down again. "Tanna," he began. I wondered if he was going to ask me to dance at that moment, but he surprised me when he said, "May I kiss you?" He caught me off guard, and I inhaled quickly. I had been wondering the same thing for days.

"Come here," he said. I surveyed the situation and realized there was no place to "come here to" but to sit on his lap. He made it easy and extended a hand to me. In the heart of the Maldives, where the turquoise and blue waters dance in harmony in the moonlight, he kissed me, taking my breath away. His arms wrapped around me, holding me close to him. His lips met mine with a gentle urgency igniting a spark that felt like a cosmic collision of stars. The salty sea breeze carried whispers of passion as time seemed to stand still, capturing the sweetness of that kiss in a timeless embrace. His lips moved from mine for an instant to hug me, then his lips were on mine again.

When he finally came up for air, he whispered in my ear, "Now I know what it's like to kiss you, and it was better than I imagined. But I think before things move too quickly, we should call it a night. Want to do this again sometime?"

"Yes I do," I said.

He stared at me, and my breathing stopped. He reached for my hand and squeezed it gently.

"I had a great time," he said.

"I had fun too." I was hoping for a little more than a hand squeeze, but I was grateful for the connection of our hands being together. We walked together to my villa, and he waited for me to go inside. I looked back. We both smiled, and he walked away.

Chapter 13

The next morning, I met Tony in line at breakfast. We ate together and laughed a lot. He held my hand as we headed to our bungalows, but we were stopped by Abbey with string in hand.

"Teach me another trick, Tanna? Please?"

If Tony and I had wanted to spend some extra time together, evidentially it wouldn't be now. Abbey walked right beside me on the boardwalk while Tony walked behind us. When we reached my bungalow, Abbey looked at Tony with that look of *why are you still here?* It made me chuckle.

Tony took my hands in his. "See you later?"

"Yes, I'll see you soon." I watched him walking away.

Abbey chimed in, "Mom and Dad said I could come to your bungalow and learn a new trick. I watched and waited for you."

"Well, we better get to teaching you. Come on in." I was slightly flattered that Abbey considered me to be the string trick specialist in all of the Maldives, but I couldn't help wishing it was Tony sitting at the kitchen table with me.

"I will show you a string trick, which is sort of like magic, which will amaze everyone you show it to." I laced the string through my fingers quickly to show her the trick. I showed her a couple of times, and then she wanted to do it on her own. That was all it took. She performed the string trick slowly, and abracadabra, the string flowed through her fingers without getting caught. She did it the second time faster.

"Great job! Now can I show you Jacob's Ladder again?"

"Of course," I said. She was getting better and faster.

I suggested that we meet again sometime where I would show her the parachute.

"Okay. You know, Mom and Dad like you."

"Oh, good I'm glad. I really like you all too."

I watched Abbey leave and waited until she was safely in her own bungalow before I closed my door. I went into my bedroom and called my daughter in Denver. It was late there, but she was a night owl and had been texting me asking how things were going. We talked for a while with the children dancing in the background and showing me their Christmas crafts. I let them know I was having fun and had found some nice people to hang with. When we hung up, I laid down and took a short nap, while a black and white movie played on the television.

When I woke up, it was already time for lunch. I hadn't made plans with Tony for lunch, so I got dressed, combed my hair, and applied a shimmery pink lipstick. Before I left, I grabbed the stone from my safe, dropping it in my bag. Today I was going to town to do some shopping, and I thought it was time to take it back to Ibrahim and see if I could get some jewelry made from it.

I didn't see any signs of movement at Tony's place. Maybe I would see him at the food court. But no, he wasn't there either. I wondered if he was working again. Abbey and her family were already eating in the food court when I walked in Abbey suddenly jumped up from her seat and headed in my direction.

"Can I eat with you? My mom and dad said it was okay with them if it was okay with you."

"Sure." I said.

Abbey found a table and proceeded to carry her tray to "our table." I finished selecting my food and sat down across from her.

"What are you doing today?" she asked.

"I'm going to town to buy something."

"Whatcha going to buy?"

"I just had the idea this morning. I am going to buy some sand shovels and pails."

"What for?"

"I'm going to buy some for the little Maldivian kids that I saw playing on the beach yesterday, and I'm going to buy one for you and one for your sister."

"Really?"

"Yes really. As soon as I finish lunch, I'm going to town." I thought she might ask if she could go with me, but she didn't. But what she did say made me feel as uneasy.

"Oh, I forgot to tell you. There were three men walking past your bungalow yesterday, over and over. They kind of walked back and forth and didn't look at the other bungalows, just yours.

I saw them from my window, so I ducked down so they couldn't see me watching them. Who were they?" Abbey asked. Then she continued. "They were short, not like my dad. I think they were from the Maldives."

My stomach plummeted. "When did you see them yesterday?"

"It was sometime in the evening when you weren't home."

She watched my face. I tried to keep a neutral expression.

"I don't know who they are. They might be looking for something they think I have, and they think it belongs to them."

"Oh, what do you have?"

"Well, I'm not really sure, maybe nothing. It's actually a long story, but could you keep an eye out for me? Will you do me a favor? Will you give me your mom's phone number? I'm going to give you mine. Because you never know what can happen, and it's good to have a few people's contact information in case we get into a jam."

Abbey waited for me to look at her and when I did, she was very excited and broke out in a little musical number for me. I was perplexed because I only wanted phone numbers, not entertainment. She smiled as she sang a little tune including her phone number, ending with "My mom's name is Sarah."

"That was darling," I said. "Can you do it again? This time I will write it down. You have a smart mom to teach you your phone number and her name like that."

She proudly sang it again and I jotted down her phone number, and I wrote down mine. "I don't want you to get involved in anything but just let me know if you see them anything unusual. And thanks for letting me know you saw them pacing up and down in front of my bungalow."

Abbey brightened. "This sounds like a detective job! Yes, I will do it."

I was grateful she was willing to keep an eye out for me, but I felt irritated that she even had to. I wanted to have the perfect vacation, but now there were three men spying on my bungalow. Couldn't I come to the Maldives and simply leave stress and worry back home? But the gemstone ... I knew that was what the three men wanted. I wasn't going to sit on the front porch of my bungalow and wave them down to come and get it. I was pretty sure they were thieves themselves, but I couldn't prove anything. I wished Tony was here so I could tell him what Abbey had just finished telling me.

As if my thoughts had summoned him, Tony walked in. What a sight for sore eyes he was. Tony pulled up a chair from the nearest table and sat on it with the back facing the table. I recited what Abbey had told me, and Abbey filled in the details.

"Do you think we need to go to the police?" I was curious.

"Right now, we don't have any evidence. The police couldn't bring them in just for walking back and forth in front of your bungalow," Tony pointed out.

"I just don't want to wait around for anything else to happen. I just feel a little edgy," I said. "Tony, Abbey is going to keep watch on my bungalow and let me know if anything strange happens."

Tony looked at Abbey. "Way to go, Abbey. You got your first detective job. Here's my number, too, just in case."

Abbey sat up a little straighter, wrote down Tony's number and beamed like a ray of sunshine.

Thank you, Tony, I thought, *for being a bright and uplifting spot in our conversation and my life.* Just having him here made me feel safer. I knew from now on he would watch my bungalow more closely along with the newly appointed Detective Abbey.

Abbey's parents were beckoning for her to come with them with a wave. Abbey's jump startled me out of my thoughts.

"I will see you later, Tanna." She ran off to dump her tray.

Tony and I watched her leave. We turned to each other at the same time. I spoke first.

"You busy today?"

He opened his hands so I could see his palms, a gesture of *I don't have a thing to do.*

"Cool, would you like to come to town and buy some kid toys with me for the little children that play on the beach? I noticed them using spoons and bowls to play in the sand. Nothing wrong with spoons and bowls, but it might be fun to have a shovel and pail and build a sandcastle. And I want to go back and ask Ibrahim if I could get some jewelry made from this stone." I patted my bag.

"Yes, that's a good idea. What do you say we get a frappe or something iced while we're there?" he suggested.

"That sounds lovely," I said.

He picked up my tray for me, and we headed for the exit.

We had barely walked out of the food court and turned the corner onto the boardwalk when we noticed Abbey running toward us.

Her little sweaty hand grabbed mine., "Hurry, it's your bungalow!" Tony and I jogged to keep up with her.

"What's wrong with my bungalow?"

"Someone has broken into it."

As we neared my bungalow, I could see the door had been opened forcefully.

"I think they used a crowbar," Tony observed as he examined the door. The onlookers walking past slowed down to get a look at the break-in.

Once again, like the first time my door was mysteriously open, Tony told me to stay outside while he checked everything out.

He didn't have to ask twice. I stood back on the main boardwalk with Abbey and her family. Tony checked every room, closet, and under the beds. I was pretty sure he wouldn't find anybody. They could have high-tailed it to Kalamazoo by now.

Tony emerged from the cottage. "No one is there," he said. "But it's a mess. Whoever had broken in tore up the place."

I approached the front door with fear in my heart. The door was wide open, and I stood in the door frame. He was right, everything was out of order and thrown like a mini cyclone had touched down in my room. All the drawers were pulled out and left open with clothes hanging down their fronts. Notepaper, Bible, and pens were strewn across the floor. My clothes were pulled out of the closet and scattered on the bed and floor. Even the top mattress was moved sideways to search for anything that might be hidden between the mattress and the box springs. Every item in my make-up purse was dumped in the tub. Luckily there was no water in the tub, and it hadn't been turned on.

Tony and I walked out together. I asked Abbey's parents if they would watch my place while we contacted security. They said they were happy to help.

The same security officer who had helped with my keycard was on duty. He smiled when we walked into his office. "What's up now?" he asked. We explained the situation to him. He alerted the receptionist that he would be attending to business at Mermaid Cove.

We walked back together, and he examined both sides of my door. He also glanced inside and saw the shambled predicament my place was in.

"I'm sorry for what happened. I don't think I can get your door to stay shut. The keycard won't work anymore. We will have to get it repaired and replace the door. I am going to go back to my office and make a call. I'll be back in a few minutes."

Abbey's parents, Sarah and Dustin, said they were really sorry for what had happened. I thanked them for watching my place. Dustin said if there was anything they could do to let them know. The family left my place and walked to their bungalow. I wished it was me walking to a place that had a working door, a floor that didn't have every inch covered with stuff, and that bad guys would stop bothering me.

I turned to Tony for the umpteenth time for help. I knew he wouldn't mind. He was always there when I needed him.

We looked again inside my bungalow. "Well, that's a fine mess we have gotten ourselves into," he joked.

I noted happily how he had phrased that *we.*

"I give it 15-20 minutes. I know we can get everything back together in that amount of time. I'll even have Siri time it for us. Hey Siri, set the timer for 17 minutes," Tony said.

"Timer is set for 17 minutes," came Siri's voice from his phone.

After straightening the beds and clearing my things off the floor, the police security knocked on our open door.

"Well, I have some good news and some not-so-good news. Your door will definitely have to be replaced. But it can't be replaced today. The person who repairs the doors will not be available until tomorrow. All the villas in the Maldives are occupied. I don't have a place for you to stay, but we can put you up in the city of Maldives. Unfortunately, it won't be as nice as these bungalows, but it's the best we can offer right now."

No more bungalow? No more casual run ins with Tony? Spending my Christmas vacation in a musty room in a motel? I could feel the cloak of despair rising above my head descending over me, and trying to push me down. I couldn't think. I wanted to scream. I couldn't scream. I closed my eyes.

Tony came to my rescue. "I have two rooms in my villa. You can stay with me."

A loud buzzing sounded. I jumped.

"Hey Siri, turn off the timer," Tony said.

"What do you say? Come to my place. We can pack all your clothes in your suitcase, and it's only four bungalows away."

I could see a pinprick of light poking through the cloud of despair. I most definitely could not see myself going to the the mainland and getting a hotel alone.

"Well, would that be too much trouble?"

"Tanna, it's no trouble at all. We can stay up, eat popcorn and watch old movies together."

That was the first time I smiled since finding someone had broken into my place. I told the security officer he did not need to find me a place. I would stay in Tony's guest room.

"Are you sure?" the security guy asked. I nodded.

I looked at Tony, whose smile lit up his eyes. Maybe this little mess wouldn't be so bad after all.

Chapter 14

Tony and I packed my clothes into suitcases and collected everything I had brought to the Maldives. We fished every piece of makeup out of the bathtub. When we arrived at his place, we placed all my things in the extra unoccupied room.

I put my clothes away for a second time and hid my suitcase in the closet. I once again flopped on the bed. I texted my kids and let them know my place had been broken into, but I was okay. Everything was fine. They wanted details, so I sent a message explaining what had happened and that Tony had a spare room I could use until tomorrow.

When I walked out of the bedroom, Tony was standing in the kitchen in his swimsuit. "You want to take a dipbefore we head to town?"

"Just give me a minute to find my swimsuit." I turned around and walked into the bedroom to change into my swimsuit. When I reappeared, we walked over and jumped into his pool.

Tony leaned against the side with his eyes closed, basking in the sun.

"Tony, there is something I forgot to tell you."

He turned his head toward me and opened his eyes.

"This morning when I went to lunch, I tossed the jewel into my bag before I walked out of my door because I wanted to take it into town."

He stared at me as if trying to figure something out.

"Well, that's a little bit of a coincidence, don't you think? I mean you take the jewel with you and thieves break in, possibly looking for it. It's lucky it wasn't there."

We sat for a moment, our heads tilted back and stared at the sky through our sunglasses.

"I'm just glad you weren't inside your cottage when they started to whack the door off with the crowbar," he said.

"Me too. Imagine if I had been inside my bungalow. I need to go back to the jeweler and get this jewel out of my hands."

"Want to swim a few laps?"

"Yes, if you swim slowly so I can keep up with you."

"Gee, I don't know, Tanna. The other day you beat me."

I grinned. "Oh yeah, I did. Okay, I'll swim slow enough for you to keep up with me."

We laughed again, pulled off our sunglasses, and leaped over the side of his pool and into the ocean. Tony and I swam together watching each other's stride to stay together.

When I could touch the bottom of the ocean, I stood up straight. I was watching his bungalow when I felt his hands touch my skin and his arms come around me from behind. I could feel his chest touching my back. My arms, which had been floating in the water, moved down and covered his arms. I breathed deeply. I felt his wet soft lips on my neck, moving across my back and to the other side of my neck. My head automatically turned in the direction of his kisses. He bent his head down and kissed my cheek, then my lips.

I could feel him turning me around to face him. We loosened our holds so his arms could maneuver around my shoulders, letting us face each other with our bodies touching, only separated by our swimwear. His lips found mine with an urgency I had never felt. With his soft lips pressed on mine, my only thought was *Don't ever let this end.* His kisses were sweetness to my body and to my soul. My heart felt like it was expanding in my chest. I could hear my breathing grow louder. Tony's hands cupped my face and then he kissed my forehead, sending pleasant shivers through me. I didn't know kisses could do that to me. His lips once again found mine.

We stopped long enough for him to look me in the eyes. "We're going to get sunburned," he said as his arms wrapped tighter around my waist.

I didn't care if I turned into a lobster, but I complied. We raced to the terrace again and climbed out of the pool feeling refreshed.

Tony suggested we take some quiet time. It had already been a long day, he said. I agreed. I took the first turn in the bathroom, quickly showered and dried off, blow dried my hair, and finally I laid down on my bed in the guest room. I didn't mean to fall sleep, but I was totally exhausted and relaxed. I woke up thirty minutes later, and I emerged from the room a new woman.

Chapter 15

When I came out, we got ready to go to town. The walk around town was warm. I had my bag with the gemstone securely on my shoulder. This time, I grabbed my wide-brimmed sky-blue hat and sunglasses. Luckily I hadn't burned while in the pool, but I didn't want to take any more chances. We walked hand in hand, took the boat trip to the mainland and went straight to the jewelers.

We talked to Ibrahim and told him what happened earlier today. He said he was glad I was safe. I told him that I went to security, but they told me I could keep it because they hadn't had any reports of anything lost, and they wouldn't be able to prove that it was contraband. I pulled out the stone and asked Ibrahim if I could get it made into some earrings and a necklace. He said he would be happy to.

Ibrahim promised they would be done before I left the Maldives. "I'll get my best men working on it immediately, ma'am," he said. "That means me," he said with a wink. I smiled.

We thanked him and went to the gift shop. Tony quickly ran back to the jewelers because he had forgotten his sunglasses.

The novelty shop was crowded with tourists looking for the cutest toy at the best price. We bought several sets of shovels and pails wrapped in thin pink nets. We took our wares with us and headed for the beach where I had spent the day reading my book the other day. Little children were playing. Tony pulled out his pocketknife and cut the net packages open, and we offered the toys to the children and opened a set for us to use, and we started building a sand castle.

The children seemed cautious at first and unsure whether they should take the toys. We sat on the sand and filled our pails with sand. We offered the remaining sets to them, and finally they took them. The extra two sets we saved for Abbey and her sister. With our set, we proceeded to fill our bucket with sand and water, then flipped over the bucket with pressed sand to carefully form the walls of the castle. Tony dug a moat and filled it with ocean water.

The children watched and sneaked glances at ours to try to make one just like it. Tony was good at sandcastles and got completely engrossed in his work, hardly looking up. When our castle was finished, we stood up and gazed our new masterpiece. Tony walked over and helped the children who were struggling. He packed the sand hard into the pails before turning them upside down. The children did the same and smiled at us. That was enough thanks for us.

We waved goodbye to the children. They waved back at us and put their hands together in a prayer-like fashion and bowed to us.

We brushed the sand off our legs and headed back to the board-walk with the pails for Abbey and her sister.

Before we caught the boat to the resort, we stopped at the ice cream shop where the aroma of waffle cones greeted us and lured us in from the sidewalk. Walking inside was like walking into a kid's heaven. We could pick our flavor and all of our toppings including sprinkles. I chose burnt almond fudge ice cream and cherry chocolate chip ice cream with real whipped cream and a cherry on top. Tony chose mint chocolate chip with cookies and cream. We sat outside at a wooden table under an umbrella.

I was deep in thought munching on my maraschino cherry and savoring my burnt almond fudge ice cream when Tony surprised me by asking in between licks of his quickly melting cone, "Would you ever consider marrying again?" He licked the melted ice cream slipping onto his cone.

I stopped licking my ice cream and swallowed my half-chewed cherry. *I would if I could marry you*, I thought, then flushed. I was grateful he couldn't read my thoughts.

I spoke slowly to Tony. "I think I would consider it someday if the right person ever came along. How about you, Tony?" I acted nonchalant but inside my heart was hammering against my chest.

"How about I answer your question with a question? Do you believe in soulmates?"

I stammered as I tried to answer him. My ice cream was threat-ening to roll down onto my hand if I didn't lick some of it off.

I held up my index finger. "Give me a sec." I licked the melting ice cream, getting it back under control.

I smiled. "Yes, I do. However, soulmates probably need to follow the same rules as others. They need to pick a mate wisely and then act kindly. Whether you marry your soulmate or not, it could be easy to turn into a nag about taking out the garbage."

Tony smiled at me. "Well put." I wanted to reach over and touch his hand with the hand that wasn't holding my melting ice cream. I wanted to let him know I felt extremely comfortable with him and felt no reservations about anything. I loved it. I could be myself, even after knowing him for such a short time. I definitely had feelings, but I was unsure what label to put on them.

"Well, if we were married," Tony said. "I'd put a little reminder in my phone about garbage day, so you wouldn't have to chase me around the house to remind me." My head started to reel. Did he just say "if we were married"? Was he planting a seed or was he being facetious? I could hardly stay focused on the conversation.

I had to work hard to hear what he was saying. "You know that special underwater restaurant with ocean life swimming all around while you eat?" I heard him say. Distractedly, I shook my head a little to clear it. "Yes, I remember. You were down in the viewing room at the same time I was. It was the second time I saw you."

"I remember you, too. I thought you looked like an interesting lady. Well, how would you like to eat at the underwater restaurant in for Christmas Eve?"

I tapped my ear to pretend I was checking my hearing. "Did I hear you right?" *The underwater restaurant? Could he be serious? For Christmas Eve dinner?*

"Yes, you did. I would like to take you out for a special evening. And for entertainment, we can enjoy all ocean life that swims by."

"How could I possibly say no?" I'd wanted to eat there since I'd first seen the pamphlet all those years ago. "But how could you get a reservation this late?"

"I got the reservation when I was in Sri Lanka. I knew that it would be busy, so it's set in stone in my name for three days from now."

We had been given cups to pop our ice cream in, upside down if needed. I flipped mine upside down and into my cup. My hands were free. I reached over to Tony, placed my hands on the sides of his face, and kissed him on the lips. "Most definitely yes."

I wasn't sure if it was the vacation romantic atmosphere or if I was actually falling in love with this man. I felt as giddy as a schoolgirl.

Tony looked at his watch. It was time to catch the boat. So we headed to the boat. The breeze from the boat was nice. It cooled my warm cheeks. I suspected it wasn't just the weather that had me a little warm.

When we got back to the resort, we walked to the boardwalk and headed to Abbey's family's villa. I knocked on the door, and Abbey answered with a bright grin, "Hi, T and T!" Then she laughed. "Do you like the nickname I came up with for you?"

"Yes, that was pretty clever." I said. Tony had the pails behind his back. I looked over at him, "We have something for you."

"Something for me?"

"Well, something for you and your sister," I answered.

"Should I get her?" Abbey asked.

"Yes, please."

Abbey yelled "Marina, come here!" It didn't take long for the bedroom door to open and for her to burst into the room.

"They have something for us," Abbey said.

"What is it?" Marina smiled shyly pulling on her hair.

Tony pulled the buckets and shovels from behind his back and handed them to both girls at the same time.

"Wow, thank you," Abbey beamed.

"Yes, thank you!" Marina said, her voice as high-pitched as Snow White's.

The girl's parents walked into the room and saw what we had given them. They thanked us and explained that they were happy they had such good neighbors while here in the Maldives.

Tony and I bounced out of their bungalow with a spring in our step, happy that we had done our good deed for the day.

Chapter 16

As we ate dinner that evening in the food court, Tony reminded me that his middle name was still "out there." He asked me if I was ready to give up and throw in the towel.

"No way," I said. He laughed.

"I will give you another clue if you like." He lured me in like a fisherman casting a net.

"I would like that." I smiled at him.

"After I tell you, will you go to the planetarium show with me tonight?"

I smiled. "Well, yes, I think that sounds like a fair trade."

"Then tomorrow will you go with me to watch for dolphins and seals?"

"Listen, honey, I would have said yes after you mentioned the planetarium show. I'd love to do all these things with you. Tony, I want to do everything." I opened my arms wide. "I want to lie on a table covered in white, poke my face through the pillow with a hole in it, and get a massage. I want to peek in the door with a rectangular window and watch the children play in the playroom with brightly colored toys. For dessert, I want a chocolate-covered cherry from the chocolate and ice cream room. I can't miss the observatory where we can see all the constellations in a brilliantly clear sky. I want to work out in the exercise room with giant machines for getting fit as a fiddle in front of a big screen TV. I want to see bioluminescence in the Indian Ocean at night."

Tony laughed with me. "Well, that's a tall order. Seems like you want to do it all."

"Yep. I have already done so much, but there's more to do. Thanks for being the best companion I could have asked for. It's been really fun. Well, minus the break in."

Tony replied, "Likewise. Yeah, break in was a real downer. But now I get to have you stay with me. I promise I'm not going to try anything," he winked at me, and a thrill went through my whole body. But he continued before I could reply. "And tomorrow your door will be fixed, and you can move back into your room."

"Thank you again for letting me stay with you. You are a perfect gentleman."

"My pleasure, my lady," he tipped an imaginary hat to me gallantly. "Let's say that if you haven't guessed my middle name by the time we have dinner in the underwater restaurant, I will tell you then in front of the fishes."

"Okay, but if I guess it before our dinner under the sea, remember your firstborn is at stake. I hope your firstborn likes … " I started to prattle.

He took my hand cutting me off. "Take me instead."

I swallowed hard. We stared at each other like no one else was around. Something in his eyes kept me staring at him. It was a sense of wonder that filled me as he gazed into my eyes with intensity. The feeling was euphoric.

Did he feel the same about me as I did about him? It felt like we were both heading in that direction. I broke the spell by lifting my glass of Cherry Coke to my lips, sucking the last few drops through the straw, and stopping when the slurping sound started.

I didn't answer his question about taking him instead of his firstborn. A wave of conflicting thoughts and feelings were raging inside of me. I wanted to desperately, but I couldn't tell if he was joking. I ran headlong into a relationship and marriage with Jeff because I took everything he said at face value, and that ended up not ending well. Besides, if he was joking or exaggerating his intentions, I didn't want to introduce any awkwardness in our relationship while I was staying with him. What if I ruined the sweetness of our courtship by seeming too eager?

Tony was talking again. I snapped back into the moment to listen. "Sorry, what did you say?" I asked.

"I said, what do you say we go back to the room before we head to the planetarium?" he asked.

"Sure." I responded.

Sitting back in Tony's kitchen, he grabbed the brochure, opened it, and reeled off the names of shows being presented at the planetarium. I couldn't help but comment on every single one. *Birth of Planet Earth* ("I really want to see that one because I always wanted to know how our planet started"), *Dark Side of the Moon* ("Ooh, that sounds mysterious"), *Pink Floyd Laser Spectacular* ("Wow, a light show?"). The fourth was *Dinosaurs of Antarctica 3D* ("I didn't know dinosaurs were there! What the H?").

He laughed and stopped me. "Yeah really, what the H? I want to see that one, too. Let's see, it starts at ..." his index finger moved down to Dinosaurs. "It starts at eight. The Pink Floyd Laser Spectacular starts right after it, we can see two."

"To kill time until the show starts, what do you say we go skinny dipping in my pool?"

"Excuse me?" I said confused but flattered.

Without even looking at me, he said, "I hope you heard me correctly. I'll repeat it. Why don't you put on your swimsuit, and we go for a nighttime swim?"

"That's what I thought you said." We both laughed.

I closed my door and came out ready for a swim. He was already in his pool. Instead of creeping in the pool toe first in degrees, I did a running jump and landed in the pool cannonball style. He watched me swim over to him and reached for my towel to get the water droplets out of my eyes.

"Tanna, I just wanted you to know I truly have fun with you. There's something special about you." I listened as I rubbed my dripping wet hair and squeezed the ends with my towel.

"Tony, I have a lot of fun with you, too. It feels so good to feel good with you."

"When I spend time with you, I have a desire to spend more time with you," he continued. "And I don't feel like I have to play games."

"I felt the same way," I agreed. It was so desirable and easy to be real. I hadn't felt this way in a relationship in a very long time, if ever. In my marriage, I struggled making sure Jeff felt good and worked desperately to meet his expectations of what he wanted me to be.

I loved the way Tony looked at me, not just a passing glance, but a look of attention, of love and longing.

Tony said. "Tanna, as you know I was married before. Are you ready to hear the story of my ex?"

Oh no, I thought. *I am I prepared for his ex-wife story? How would I measure up to this most important relationship in his life?* But I wanted to hear it because I had given Tony the full version of my failed marriage, and I knew this would give me a window into his character and his life. He gazed out into the ocean searching the horizon like it might help him communicate better what he was feeling.

"I loved Beth. She was a good person. She was creative and charitable. We grew up together, and our families always assumed we would get married. Eventually, it made sense for us, and we did get married. We were very young. I thought we were happy. But as the kids grew up and left the house, we slowly drifted apart. I got the feeling that maybe we didn't have much in common after all. There was a lot of pressure from our town and from our families for us to get married, but I don't know if we were ever truly in love. Not in the way I imagine love is now.

"Over time, we slowly realized that we didn't have the same goals anymore. She became really involved with her work. I supported that, but I think spending so much time apart made us realize that we actually liked being friends more than being married to each other. The things that brought us together in the beginning weren't there anymore.

"For me, something was missing. I had felt a love or what I thought was love somewhere back in my life, but it definitely wasn't there with her anymore. I spent a long time being sad about it, but eventually we mutually decided that we could stay friends and be in our children's lives, but we weren't going to try to force the marriage to work anymore. The marriage felt like a puzzle piece that almost fit and a few quick taps with the mallet would force it into place.

"She was the one who finally suggested we separate. Although I stressed for a while about whether or not it was the right decision, eventually, something interesting happened. Every day I started to feel less burdened, a little bit like you when you thought of divorce. A lightness came. The thought of going back and trying to make it work made me depressed. What is interesting is neither one of us had someone else who was waiting in the wings with open arms. But it became very clear to me that we had made the right choice."

We didn't talk for a minute, and I was glad. I wanted to process what he had said.

"How do you feel now, Tony?" I finally asked.

"It's been eight years since we divorced, and I think both of us are happier. In fact, I truly wish her all the best. She's remarried, by the way. She married a used car salesman, and she's never been happier," he concluded.

"Thanks for telling me all of that. It means a lot that you trust me with all of that." There was something so freeing about hearing his story. No drama, no hard feelings, no one I needed to compare myself to. It made me be brave. "Do you want to know how I feel about you, Tony?"

Excitement sparkled in his eyes. "Yes, I do."

I splashed water at him and raced to the other side of his pool.

He swam after me, catching me by the shoulder. He spun me around, wrapped his arms around me, and kissed me with his soft lips first on my forehead, sliding onto my temple, my cheek, and finally, my waiting lips.

I felt elated with my arms tingling all the way to my fingertips. This was a new love I hadn't felt before, but I liked it. We got out of the pool. With his arm around my shoulder and my arm around his waist, we walked back inside.

Chapter 17

Sitting in the domed theater with the lights off, we slid into our seats. The shows were incredible. The animation danced along the walls and ceiling of the theatre. It was immersive. It almost seemed like we were surrounded by dinosaurs on all sides. I felt like I was a character in the story they told with music, lights, and stunningly rendered visuals. I had been going to the movie theatre by myself for the last year as a way to get out of my house, and it made a huge difference to have someone to share this experience with. The second show started with my head on Tony's shoulder and his arm around me.

As the show ended, everyone got out of their seats and talked about how amazing the light show and music were. I heard Abbey yelling above the din, "Tanna! Tanna!" I turned around to her whole family waving at us with big smiles. We waved back.

We walked back along the boardwalk with Abbey's family. Talking to Sarah and Dustin reminded me of the long days and nights of raising little ones, and the multiple stresses that appeared on a daily basis.

"You have such a nice family. You guys are doing great raising your kids. Abbey and Marina are darling girls. I sometimes miss the days when my children were young, but having my little grandkids helps," I said.

Dustin said he was glad that we all were neighbors in Maldives. We agreed.

Tony and I waited for them to enter their villa before we went into his. I hadn't realized how tired I was until I sat down at the kitchen table with my elbows planted firmly on the table and both hands holding up my head. When he suggested a game of checkers, I dropped my arms dramatically, collapsed them like dominos, and I rested my head on his table in feigned exhaustion.

"Give me a minute while I brush my teeth and wash the sun, sweat, and sand off my face." I got up and went to the large shared bathroom. There were two round mirrors above a large double sink. The counters were marble, and everything seemed to sparkle in the chandelier light. I didn't realize bungalows came with such luxurious bathrooms. It included a rain shower, and a deep tub faced a large window that looked out onto the ocean view. I had just set my toothbrush down on the counter when I saw Tony's reflection in the mirror. He stood at the doorway. I smiled at him. "Mind if I come in?" he asked.

"Not at all. I was just about to wash my face."

"Maybe I can help?" he asked politely.

"Sure," I said, my heart beating a bit faster.

He took the washcloth out of my hand, rinsed it with cool water, and wrung it. He looked at me, lifted my hair from off my neck, and wiped the sand and sweat from my warm skin. He stood beside me, after rinsing the cloth and wringing it out again, he slid it up and down my right arm and then the left, sending pleasant tingles down my arm. Then he dabbed the washcloth on my face, cooling every square inch it touched except my warm cheeks, which blushed beneath his gaze despite my best intentions to seem calm and collected. I guess that wasn't in the cards.

When he stopped with the washing, I opened my eyes. We stared at each other. It was a moment when I felt lost in time and space. The only thing that existed was him, me, and my loudly beating heart. I had felt it before and now it was here again.

"I will meet you in the living room," I said. "I want to get into my pajamas before we start playing."

"Sure thing. That will give me a chance to get ready for bed too. Hope you don't mind a matching Superman pajama set." He winked at me.

"Actually I prefer it," I laughed.

After walking into my bedroom, I changed into my comfortable loose pajama pants with an elastic waistband. It was nice not to have the pressure to be sexy in this setting. It wasn't something I was ready for, and I wanted to be comfortable with Tony. I wanted to show him the real me, not some made up version. So he was going to see me without makeup, in baggy pajamas and everything. Upon returning to the kitchen, the checkerboard was set up and Tony was waiting, freshly washed and Superman pajamas on.

"Are you ready for a friendly game of checkers, my lady?"

"Absolutely. I should warn you. I'm the best checkers player west of the Mississippi, and I feel like you are going to get beat tonight," I said with a sly smile.

"Oh really? I had no idea I was in the company of such a legend," he retorted. "Well, you didn't know that you were going up against the best checkers player east of the Mississippi. You've met your match, Tanna Lewis."

I sat opposite Tony with my elbows on the table staring at the checkerboard. I was red. He was black. The first few moves were easy as we pushed forward trying to king our men and nab a few of each other's pieces along the way. It became clear rather quickly that neither of us knew how to play very well—his bluff was as good as mine—but we were well matched in our abilities. Little piles of both red and black started to stack on either side of the board.

We got lost in conversation, jokes, and quoting our favorite movies. I thought I could use a brief moment of strategy to turn the game in my favor. I told Tony to look outside at the gorgeous moon. As he looked away, I moved my piece, hoping he wouldn't notice where I had placed it. I didn't want to cheat, but how else was I going to win?

"That's really nice," he said.

When he looked back at the board, he laughed. He proceeded to jump two of my pieces. I reached over, grabbed his arm, and said, "Hold on there, Tex, that isn't in the rules."

He laughed. "Last time I played checkers, it was totally legal. I'm going to have to watch you."

I could feel the weight of my eyelids getting heavier. I laid my head on my arm on the table with both eyes open to let him know I was totally awake and watching his moves very closely. When I counted only three of my red pieces remaining, I knew it would be hard to beat him.

"Hey wake up, sleepyhead, it's your turn."

I jumped to attention. I tried to concentrate, but within two moves, one more of my red pieces left the board. I was beat. It was about time too. I was exhausted.

Tony came over to my side of the table and offered me a handshake. He helped me stand up, put his arm around me, and guided me.

"Do you need help making it to your bed before you fall asleep?" he asked.

"No, I think I can make it from here. Thanks for a wonderful day. Goodnight, Tony." I kissed him on the cheek.

"Goodnight, my Tanna."

Chapter 18

The next morning, I woke late. Tony wasn't anywhere in sight, but a note was waiting for me on the kitchen table where the checkerboard had been. I picked it up to read, "Had to leave for a few minutes—meet me at the food court for breakfast."

I dressed leisurely, applied my makeup, combed my hair, and read text messages from my kids who were checking in on me. I texted them back, catching them up on all the events so far and wished them a good day.

The food court was crowded with the usual hungry guests, except I didn't see Tony anywhere. I opted for a warm comforting breakfast of oatmeal topped with blueberries, brown sugar, and granola. I also picked up a square of breakfast casserole made of eggs, hash browns, sausage topped with cheese, and a slice of toast. I chose a table big enough for two and positioned myself so I could see anyone who walked into the food court.

Suddenly, two of the men I suspected were thieves walked into the food court. They paid no attention to the line of guests, pushing and butting past everyone rather rudely. They stopped and looked around. One of them looked in my direction and elbowed the other. He pointed right at me! It was a scene out of a thriller movie, and I was the lead. My heart raced as they started walking towards me.

Where is Tony? Are these men going to mug me? Where is the third man? Are they looking for the jewel? I don't even have it with me! It's at the jewelers, I thought. I decided to make it look like I had it. I didn't want to endanger Ibrahim by telling them where the jewel actually was. So I stood up and positioned my bag over my shoulder opposite them, clutching the fabric handles tightly. My heart was racing frantically.

I heard a little girl's voice yell my name. I didn't look away from the two men, but I knew it was Abbey.

They approached my table walking fast and one of them pulled out a knife from inside his coat. My stomach constricted and fear and adrenaline pumped through my body making everything go quiet. A third man came from behind me. He held his arms straight out in front of him with something in his hands. It was Tony holding a gun. My fluttering heart almost stopped. *What was Tony doing with a gun?*

"Stop right there!" Tony yelled with authority. The two men abruptly turned around. "Everybody else get outside!" Tony yelled to the room. "Put your hands up! On your knees!" Two security officers came running into the room. Tony stepped aside while the two security guards handcuffed the men with their hands behind their backs.

"Thanks, Tony," one of the security guys said. The situation seemed to be getting under control as the security guards marched the two guys out of the room. I thought the craziness was over until one of the men in cuffs turned around. One of the men said in a heavy accent, "You better give it to us or else." The hateful scowl on his face sent a shock wave through me.

Tony pointed at the chair opposite mine. "May I?"

"Of course," I said a bit breathlessly. "But you have some explaining to do."

"First, I'm going to run and grab some breakfast. Be right back. Save my seat."

I looked at my white knuckles clutching my bag. I loosened my grip on the handles and a healthy pink sprang back into them. Many questions zoomed around in my head at once, and I wondered which one to ask first. *Why did Tony have a gun? Why did the security officers seem to be fine with him having a gun? Why did they know his name? What would the men have done to me to get the jewel? Was I safe? Did they know I was staying with Tony?*

Abbey and her family returned to the food court and walked up to our table. "Tanna, are you okay?" Abbey asked. "We saw what happened, and we were scared for you. What did those men want?"

"I'm fine. Thanks for stopping by. Have you eaten?" I tried to steer the conversation away from what had happened. I wasn't ready to answer all of their questions right now.

"No," Sarah said. "We're getting in line right now."

"Well, the food is wonderful as usual." I gestured to the food at my table.

Abbey and Marina waved goodbye as the family moved toward the line for breakfast.

Tony finally arrived. He seemed totally relaxed. Before he had a chance to sit down, I started asking him rapid-fire questions.

"Hold it," he said holding up a hand. "I will answer all your questions, but let me sit down and get a sip of coffee first."

I waited impatiently for him to sip his coffee.

"Tanna, I know you have a lot of questions," Tony said casually. "And I will answer all of them. But first, do you remember when I said I worked for the government?"

"Yes, I remember. Why do you have a gun? I assumed you had some desk job, but now you've got me questioning everything. I mean, don't get me wrong; I was glad you had a gun a few minutes ago, but your job requires you to carry a weapon? I mean, do you need a gun to help people get visas to come to America?" I was shocked.

He waited for a moment while he smothered grape jam on his toast and took a bite.

He moved his head closer to me and spoke in a whisper. "I work for the State Department."

He waited for me to take that piece of information in as he spooned a large helping of salsa onto his scrambled egg.

"Tony how did it all come about?"

"My uncle worked in DC for the State Department, and I always listened to him as a kid and respected him. I could see the good that he did and how much he enjoyed his work, and I wanted to do something similar with my life. So I made up my mind and got the training I needed to do it." He took another bite of his eggs.

I looked at him and whispered, "Are you a spy or something? Can you tell me more, or if you do, will you have to kill me?" We both shared a laugh.

"I can tell you, Tanna. I work as a Foreign Service Specialist. I serve for America's interests internationally and help prevent crime around the world." He went on, dropping his voice even lower. "To make a long story short, my department keeps tabs on what is going on around the world and shares information with international agencies. They employ people like me to help gather that information and share it with our allies around the world. We help prevent crime according to international law."

He stopped talking. I waited for him to go on with his speech, which I wasn't particularly understanding, but he seemed to reach the end.

"Basically, we are a network around the world protecting it with a lot of other agents working to keep terror down and countries safe," he said.

"Wow." I downed the last of my orange juice. I thought back on my experiences with Tony. He always acted calm in the face of chaos. He had known who to call when I had my little calamity with the door. He happened to show up at the jewelry shop. Had he been carrying his gun then?

"Were you carrying a gun when we were at the jewelry shop? You know, when I was showing my gem to the jeweler?"

He squinted his eyes and waited a long five seconds. "Yes."

My memories went to when Tony had come into the jewelry shop, the day I had brought my jewel to let the jeweler see it. I didn't recall seeing a gun, a holster, or any evidence that he was totting a gun.

"I can say after everything that has happened since I found that jewel, it's been a comfort to have you with me."

"Tanna, it was always my pleasure to protect you. You remind me of someone." His voice trailed off. I waited expectantly, but he didn't clarify.

I hoped he wasn't going to say I reminded him of his mother, even though his mom was probably a wonderful person. I wanted to be seen as separate from any maternal figures in his life. So I switched topics. "Were you really helping people in Sri Lanka get visas to come to the USA?"

"Yes, I was. I actually did both. I helped people get visas and worked closely with the US Embassy to eliminate potential problems, just like a few minutes ago when those men were trying to grab your bag. I am in close contact with the security guards here, which is why they know my name." He paused for a second to drink some more coffee and switched to another topic.

"So, Tanna. I talked to the guards and found out your door will be fixed by noon. That's about two hours away. If you like I can help you move your stuff back, or ..." he made some low mumbling noises under his breath.

"What'd you say?" I asked.

"Oh, nothing."

I knew I didn't want to go back and stay in my bungalow alone just yet. So much had happened since I checked in at this resort, and the more time I spent with Tony, the safer I felt. My thoughts quickly turned to how grateful I was I'd gotten to meet this incredible man.

The thought made me laugh because I was still learning all sorts of things about him. We stood up at the same time and carried our empty plates on trays to the food drop-off area.

"Do you have plans for this afternoon?" he asked me on the way out of the food court.

"Well, you said you wanted to go swim with the dolphins and take a bus trip around the Maldives with me. Still want to go?"

"Absolutely," he said.

"How about we get the boat into the Maldives and then on the way back, swim with the dolphins? The bus trip is only about forty-five minutes. Swimming with the dolphins will take about an hour. We have time for both."

We went back to the villa and packed a bag with all the things necessary like swimsuits, flip flops, chap stick, towels, sunglasses and sunscreen. One thing I didn't want was a red blistering sunburn that ached whenever I raised an eyebrow.

Chapter 19

The clouds darkened the sky, and I was grateful the rain pounded down on the little bus and not on our heads. The tour guide, Joseph, told us that the Maldives atolls were formed from extinct prehistoric volcanoes in the Indian Ocean. When the ocean floor subsided with the volcano, corals began to populate and grow around it, forming a fringed reef. As time passed, the reef slowly became a barrier reef enclosing a shallow lagoon inside. The Maldives has a history that goes back 2,550 years and its name means the garland of islands, though the country was founded in July of 1965.

Joseph continued. He told us the chain of Maldives islands were made of 1,900 small coral islands and sandbanks. Many of the islands were still inhabited. The guide said that by 2050 possibly 80% of the islands would be underwater because of climate change and other factors. Some had already been taken back by the sea. How sad!

He said, "You can own an island for as little as $35,000." I imagined myself selling my house and living here and owning an island.

I wondered if the novelty of living in this paradise would wear off. Would I live here for a while and would my opinion change? Would I want to sell my island and yearn to go back to the USA? It seemed hard to believe now, but I knew in my heart that I would miss my kids and grandkids far too much.

We drove through the small city on a bus and saw homes with children playing out in the rain-soaked dirt right in their front yards. We saw food markets advertising fish and other popular Maldivian foods.

Our guide informed us that it was less expensive to live in the Maldives than in the United States. He told us the capital of the Maldives was called Male. The majority of the Maldivian people were Muslim, and the main food was fish.

One of the guests asked the question, "What are the Maldives known for?"

He proudly answered, "We are known for our clear emerald waters, beautiful beaches that stretch as far as the eye can see, and of course luxurious overwater bungalows."

As I was turning to Tony to tell him I could have answered that question easily, he reached for my hand. My lips moved close to his ear so he could hear me above the tour guide on the microphone and the rain pelting the top of the bus. To punctuate the sentence, I left a soft kiss on his cheek. He turned to me and smiled. I knew he would have kissed me back and not on the cheek if other guests were not present.

The tour ended and so did the rain. It was a beautiful time of day for swimming with the dolphins and seals. Tony and I took turns changing to swimming attire in the closest restroom after our bus came to a complete stop.

We waited fifteen minutes and boarded a small boat called a SeaFarer. With the Maldives dolphin sunset cruise, the boat excursion had become popular in recent months and more so with dinner and drinks being served. Tony had purchased tickets for the Maldivian bus tour and the boat tour with dolphins at the same time.

Sitting on the edge of the boat, we watched the surface of the waters. The dolphins must have known we came for a show, and they didn't disappoint. Their playful antics and chirping sounds were delightful to experience firsthand. They leaped in the air, frolicked, and played. They made clicking sounds in rapid sequence, called click trains.

We were going to get in the water and swim with these smooth sleek creatures, but we changed our minds and decided to watch these magnificent dolphins from the side of our boat. We knew, even if we had donned snorkel gear and fins, and they gave us a head start, we would be no match for these swimmers that were born to swim at high speeds. Soon some seals arrived to join the party. I'd forever remember the dolphins arching high into the air and diving back into the ocean. We watched until daylight turned into dusk. That was the point when the wildlife entertained us no more and swam into deeper waters.

For dinner, we had local dishes of yellow curry, potatoes, and onions served over rice. Pineapple and coconut slices were on a separate plate. A fish soup with a tomato base was mildly spicy. For dessert, a large dollop of orange mango ice cream was served.

I sat across from Tony sipping Cherry Coke over ice. I thought about the food we had eaten and marveled at the recipes of how to make them. Maybe I needed to blog about this trip after all. I had no idea the food would be so exceptional. Good thing I had been taking pictures of my food all week. I tried to recreate the recipes, imagining how it possibly could have taken 100 years to perfect them, or even longer. How the flavors were so perfectly married together. None of the flavors begged for attention but were very content to mix well and please our taste buds. Tony's favorite was the yellow curry over rice, as was mine. As we ate, we watched the tiny ripples of water shining like silver from the waxing gibbous moon.

I didn't have a care in the world, except the desire to feel like this forever. I felt like I had found the perfect man, the perfect atmosphere, the perfect food, and the perfect feeling. I had even stopped thinking about the men who had charged at me in the food court and broken my room door with a crowbar. Even the incident in the jewelry shop was fading like rain washing away a chalk picture.

As we were talking, Tony brought up the possibility of buying and maintaining an Airbnb. I thought he was talking about here in the Maldives. We had been talking about how nice it would be to live here. And then I got distracted by the dolphins and must have missed something. He questioned how much it would cost and whether it be easier to get a property manager to attend to all the details, where the best location would be, how close to the beach, and whether I knew the name of a good local property management agency. It took me a minute before I thought I understood him wrong.

"Wait, where are you looking to buy something?" I inquired.

"Where else? Right in your home state of California. Owning an Airbnb has been an interest to me for quite some time."

He was serious. He had already been online looking at duplexes, checking to see which areas allowed short-term rentals, the cost of buying one, and what was involved in maintaining one. He was excited about having it somewhere close to the water and maybe a 20 to 30-minute drive to Disneyland. Vacationers would love it.

Two lights went on in my head. The first little bulb that glistened was the thought that I could manage his Airbnb. I had always enjoyed the thought of furnishing and decorating a condo, then renting it or selling it. I had owned a condo in the past and done that very thing. The second little bulb grew brighter when I started thinking about the evening Tony had planned for us in the underwater restaurant the day after tomorrow. It was something to look forward to.

Of course, every event that I had experienced in the Maldives was something to look forward to, but the dinner under the sea would be the crème de la crème. It was the one thing on my list of things that I wanted to do that I didn't have a plan for before Tony invited me. It was going to be the most special date of my life with the most special person I'd ever met. Plus, he would reveal his middle name if I had not already guessed it. I couldn't wait.

I heard the boat's motor shut off and go silent. Tony stepped down the stairs first and reached his hand to help me down the stairs and onto dry land.

The old English lanterns sitting on the edges of the boardwalk glowed with a dim pale yellow light, and between each one was a string of very tiny white fairy lights. Tony and I walked straight to the registration building and asked for security. Tony and the security guard exchanged hellos. My keycard was handed to me in a white envelope with my name on it.

"Sorry for the inconvenience," the security guard apologized.

I told Tony I had a video call arranged with my daughter Ruby in one hour. He said that was fine and maybe we could meet tomorrow and go to the observatory. He helped me lug my suitcases over to my Mermaid Cove bungalow. I dropped my bag, and he brought my suitcase inside.

"Thank you, Tony. I had so much fun today. I enjoyed it all so much."

"Hey, it was all my pleasure. I had a great time too." We kissed in the moonlight. I didn't care if Abbey or anyone else was peeking at us.

My grandkids danced in front of the cameras on the video call. Both of them crossed their eyes at each other, walking stiff like zombies. I laughed out loud. It was great to see them again and know that they were doing well. They asked me if I swam in the ocean too much, would I develop gills? My granddaughter wanted to tell me her newest joke for her new standup routine.

"Ok, Grandma," she said, "Did you hear about the fish that decided to sign up for a triathlon?"

"No."

"He did it for the halibut." The children screamed with laughter.

Ruby told me what they were doing and promised to come to Sunday dinner when I returned home, and we shared air kisses and hung up.

I separated the two clean white sheets on my bed and crawled in. I thought of Tony in his room. Was he thinking about me? Because I sure was thinking about him. I mentally asked the Universe to give me a hint of his middle name, so I could solve it and impress him before our big dinner. I was having a hard time waiting. It would be the sweet icing on the cake if I could get him and not his firstborn. That was a deal I could live with.

Chapter 20

I woke up to Abbey beating on my door.

"Tanna! Tanna! Are you home?"

I looked at my watch. 9:30am. I didn't realize I slept in so late. "Just a minute," I called, my voice croaking. I got up quickly and put on my robe.

I stumbled my way sleepily to the door and opened it rubbing my eyes. "Hi," I said.

"Hi Tanna, can we do more string tricks?" Abbey asked gleefully.

"Sure, but I need to get ready first, and I haven't eaten breakfast yet."

"Oh, we already ate," she said.

"How about I go eat and then come to your house, and we can do more string tricks together?"

"Okay, I'll watch for you."

I showered and got dressed in floral shorts and a white top. After washing my face, brushing my teeth, and combing my hair, I was out the door. It was close to 10am. The food court would close soon.

Tony's bungalow was a few steps away, and I couldn't resist. I walked up to his door and knocked three times. He wasn't there, so I walked by myself to the food court.

The food court had a few people but most had eaten and left already. There was hot food still under the lights with warmers underneath. I selected a dish of chunked-up sweet potatoes with a fried egg on top and avocados on the side. I grabbed the sriracha sauce as I walked to my table. I selected bright pink cranberry juice and coffee with two slices of wheat toast. I ate quickly, knowing Abbey was waiting, placing my two mini chocolate croissants in my napkin as I walked out.

I arrived at Abbey's to find the door was open. She was waiting for me. We sat down at the kitchen table, and I pulled out a mini croissant for her.

"Oh, thanks," she said,

Her string was already on the kitchen table, plus another one she had cut for me. We reviewed Jacob's Ladder, which she had mastered. I showed her the magic string trick, where you wind the string around your fingers. The magic comes when you pull it from thumb to pinky without it getting caught. She learned it quickly. The parachute was equally easy. I then taught her how to play string games with a partner.

"I can't wait to show Mom and Dad!" she squealed when we'd finished.

"Okay, well I need to get going. I'll see you later."

"See you later, Tanna! Thanks for your help and for the croissant." Abbey really was a sweet girl.

I walked past Tony's bungalow and knocked on the door again. I waited for a minute, and when he didn't show, I headed for my own bungalow. I had already booked the morning with exercise on the exercise machines and a massage afterward. I dressed in shorts, sneakers, and an aqua t-shirt with a gorgeous large turtle on the front.

The large exercise balls, treadmills, and work benches were indoors with some equipment outside. I wanted to be inside, out of the sun. I moved from machine to machine for about an hour before I went to my massage appointment.

Upon arriving at the spa for the second time this vacation, I found a peaceful room that always had a view of the ocean that was especially reserved for massages. The bed was vacant, and my masseuse invited me to come in and put my baggage on a shelf. I laid down, placing my head in the white cutout.

During my massage, with her magic fingers kneading my back, I traveled deep into the Universe, stood back from the spiral Milky Way, and saw my planet on one of the spiral arms, located two-thirds of the way out from the center of the galaxy. It was my home. It was beautiful and the only planet I knew anything about. I came close to a black hole but didn't go in. I went further out into space where the sun didn't shine. Dark matter was visible or maybe I simply felt it. I didn't stay long in dark matter, for it felt mysterious, unknown, and scary.

I came back into the light from the sun, opened one eye, and saw our ocean. I was grateful to be a guest on planet Earth for a few years. In my mind's eye, I soared to Mars and stood by the rover named *Opportunity*, which was one of the five that were lucky enough to roll around on Mars. The surface was red and lumpy with mountains and valleys, like an orange if it were bigger. I loved how my imagination could go from planet Mars to deep in the ocean where light began to dwindle. I had a very active imagination and a deep spirit.

Then I was with my precious grandchildren watching them laugh with each other, and my precious children. I saw my mom and dad walking on a sidewalk holding hands. I saw my sisters, brother, and their families which made me smile. My ex-husband came into view for all of two seconds. I realized I didn't hate him. For the first time, when I thought about Jeff, I felt totally neutral. I could wish him well and forget the pain he had caused me.

I switched views to Tony. What a sharp contrast. Thinking about Tony there were definitely positive feelings involved. At that point, I could hardly wait to get to the sauna, take a shower, and find that man.

The tiny white cooking timer rang, and the masseuse's hands left my back. I thanked her, and she bowed.

"Namaste," she said.

After the sauna, I headed to lunch, but the food court was closed. I went to my room and pulled out the room service menu from the desk drawer, called the number, and ordered a chicken croissant sandwich, veggies and dip, and a Vietnamese blended coffee with boba balls.

As I ate, I watched an American movie called *Rebecca*. Sir Laurence Olivier and Joan Fontaine lit up the black and white 1940s screen with all the glamour, glitz, and fashion. I had seen it many times and loved it every time.

I ate half a sandwich, some veggies, all my boba drink, and put the food onto the tray on the floor. Then I went and took a cat nap.

I awoke to someone knocking on my door. Looking in the mirror, I hoped there were no marks from the blanket embedded in my face.

It was Tony. "Hey Tanna. I came by to see if you want to go to the observatory after dinner tonight."

"Yes, I do." It was something we hadn't done yet. My mind was starting to race to make sure I hadn't missed anything.

"So, dinner and then the observatory?"

"Okay." I said.

"I have a few things to do first. Can I pick you up at about six?"

I nodded. "Sounds good."

He squeezed my hands with his, kissed me on the mouth, and was gone.

I changed into my swimsuit, grabbed my towel, hat, and sunscreen, and headed out the door to my pool. As I sat in my pool, I could see two giggling girls I recognized standing on a porch a few bungalows away.

"Can we play in your pool?" Abbey called. I waved them over.

I hopped out, opened my front door and let them come to the pool. They hopped in, splashing water on my sunglasses with every kick they made. I closed my eyes and let them play. Up until they roped me into a round of Marco Polo.

"Hey, do you two want to come inside and get an ice-cold water or would you like your water out here?" I asked when we'd finished playing.

They looked at each other. "Out here."

"I'll be right back."

I walked inside with a smile on my face, filled three tall glasses with water and ice, and brought them back outside.

"Come and get it," I said. I sat one of the glasses down on the step.

They both swam close to my feet. I turned the glasses upside down on their heads.

They shrieked with delight.

"Tanna, that's cold," Abbey said.

"Want to get me back?"

"Yes!" They screamed. Together, they grabbed the glass of water and poured it on my head.

I shrieked like a baby wolf. "Wow, I didn't think it would be that cold."

The girls laughed. They stayed and played until Sarah summoned them. They left my pool with a "Thanks for letting us play, Tanna!"

"You're welcome, come back again sometime," I said.

I was alone in my pool with my thoughts and a few small ice chunks floating around. Tomorrow night was my big date with Tony to eat at the restaurant under the sea. I still didn't have a hint of what his middle name was. But a different image occupied my thoughts: Tony on one knee with a ring. What if this big date was really a set up to ask me to marry him?

It was a shocking thought, but I liked it. I had known pretty much the whole time I had known Tony that I could marry and live with him. I felt compatible with him, but there was something larger that felt right when I was with him. The world just seemed right when we were together. I felt at peace. I was over fifty—it didn't take long for me to realize that peace was something that doesn't come around all the time. When I was younger, it probably would have taken longer to realize the significance of that peace. I knew better now.

I looked at my watch and realized I needed to hurry if I was going to make it to town before my dinner with Tony. I had been window shopping for Christmas gifts for my family all week, and I had found what I wanted. Today was my day to go purchase them. I threw on a flowered sundress with white lace on the neck and sleeves.

In town, the Maldives Bazaar held everything you would ever want to tote home. I selected vanilla coconut hand cream for my daughters along with a bottle of real vanilla for cooking. For their husbands, I chose Luis Vuitton's "Imagination" cologne. For the grandchildren, I selected ocean themed t-shirts and some sea creature figurines. With the gifts purchased, that was one more thing I could cross off my list before going home back to the States.

After showering and making myself presentable, I waited for Tony. He was prompt and I invited him in.

"You hungry?" he asked.

"I am—hungry as a bear."

"Well, let's get out here then."

On the way to the food court, he inquired if I was excited about going to the special underwater dinner tomorrow.

"Yes, I am, and for dessert, I can find out your middle name."

"Oh yeah. If you don't guess it by tomorrow, I'll tell you. That was the deal."

Tonight I was in the mood for a wedge salad with garlic bread sticks, with cherry pie á la mode for dessert. Tony selected roast beef with potatoes, gravy, and corn on the cob with apple pie á la mode for dessert.

Tony led the conversation this evening. He wanted to know more about my life. He inquired further about my childhood, my parents, my siblings, and my kids. We sat at the table for close to two hours.

I did my best to turn the conversation to him. "I still want to know more about you. Even though I don't know everything about you, I think I know the important stuff, like you're a really good person. You help people all the time by getting them visas, and you belong to the State Department trying to fight crime and terrorism around the world. I don't have to know all the facts to know that you are someone with integrity who loves to help people."

"Thank you, Tanna. That's really nice of you to say those things. I feel the same as you. I got a lot of facts, but down deep, I know you. I know your spirit. I know you are a good person and someone I love being with." I could honestly say, I felt the same way. It was like our souls knew each other from another life. He grabbed my tray, took them away, and came back hand outstretched to help me up. Always the perfect southern gentleman.

With the sun setting, we walked to the observatory hand in hand. As with most things in the Maldives, reservations were required. Luckily Tony had that covered. He whipped out two passes from his wallet. We were each led to a telescope. Each of us had a guide to show us where to look and what we were looking at. As I looked at the nighttime sky, I marveled at its vast greatness, going on forever and ever.

I took my eyes off the telescope and gazed at the ocean, which looked fluorescent blue. I asked the guide why that was. He said they named it the *Sea of Stars*, also called bioluminescence. He said the glow of the light we saw was actually emitted from living creatures, which has sea plankton present in it. The creatures emit light, which is only seen in the dark of night. Microorganisms and microbes produce a lively glow, which disorients predators.

This process personifies the beauty of the beach at night. He said some people come here just to see this impressive phenomenon. It totally looked like stars were in the ocean. I looked again through the telescope. We eyeballed the nighttime sky for a total of ten min-utes and stared at the ocean as we walked back to our bungalows.

Tony kissed me long and tenderly. I wouldn't have wanted to miss the meeting of our lips that night for anything. Everything felt magical. I wanted more, but Tony said he had some things he had to take care of. *Why did he often seem so busy taking care of things while on vacation?* I wanted those things he needed to take care of to be me. But I understood he had other obligations. I said good night as our lips and bodies separated.

Chapter 21

This morning in the Maldives was especially beautiful for a morning swim. It was Christmas Eve, and it would be my last day and night here. I pulled on my polka dot two-piece swimsuit, and walked over to my pool.

I had barely sat down on the edge when I saw the other thief on the boardwalk leaning over so he could see me. "Give me the jewel, now," he shouted.

I froze, not knowing what to do. But I didn't have the jewel. "I don't have it," I said as calmly as I could muster.

"You're lying. We saw you take it out of the water. The jewel is ours, now give it to me!" he argued.

I hoped he wouldn't find a way to the pool through my house to drown me. But then, if he drowned me, he wouldn't be able to get information about the jewel.

Tony, help me. I prayed silently. Just then, I saw Abbey staring out her window with a cell phone in her hand. She must have heard the man on the boardwalk yelling at me.

Bless her heart, she was watching out for me. I hoped she was calling Tony because I needed his help right now.

A split second later, I heard Tony's voice. "Put your hands up." The man turned and swung at Tony. Tony ducked, grabbed the thief's arm, spun around, and pinned the thief's arm behind him. He reached up, grabbed the other arm, and held the thief in a strong hold. Before Tony could call for backup, two security guards appeared on the scene, and each one pulled out a set of handcuffs.

"Thanks Tony," one of the officers said. "We'll take it from here. Looks like we've found all the jewel thieves we've been looking for."

If looks could kill, I surely would have been dead from the glare the thief shot at me. The security guards escorted the man toward the end of the boardwalk, where two police cars were waiting with flashing red lights.

Tony called out from the boardwalk, "Hey, you okay?

I nodded.

"Care for some company?"

I didn't have words, only that I wanted to be in his arms. I got out of my pool dripping wet, opened my front door for him, and went into his waiting arms. He gathered me up. We didn't miss a beat but walked straight to my pool and sat in the water, me in my swimsuit and Tony in his shorts and shirt.

"Tony, I was so scared."

"I know, darling."

I felt a tap on my shoulder. It was Abbey—my little savior who had called Tony. She had followed us to the pool. She sat on the edge. Without saying a word, she hugged me from the other side.

"Abbey, you're amazing and wonderful. Thank you for calling Tony."

"I saw that man hanging around, and my dad called the security guards right away," Abbey said. "He told me to call Tony."

"You did a brave thing, Abbey," Tony said.

We were all silent for a moment and then Abbey blurted out, "I know a secret!"

"What is it?"

"Well, if I tell you, it won't be a secret anymore," Abbey confessed, sounding proud.

"I guess that's two secrets I don't know the answer to." I said. "Your middle name and Abbey's secret."

Tony said, "You'll find out both soon enough."

"Now what's that supposed to mean?" I asked.

Abbey jumped out of the water with a monstrous smile on her face and stared first at Tony and then at me.

"Bye."

"Bye, Abbey."

"How about I order us some breakfast to be delivered to Mermaid Cove, and we can eat at your pool?" Tony offered.

I nodded. He ordered two hot breakfasts to be delivered to my bungalow.

He asked to borrow my keycard and said he would be right back. After his phone call, he grabbed his gun and walked to his bungalow and changed into swim trunks.

We sat in my pool, and I closed my eyes under my sunglasses. The breakfast was enough to keep the wolf of hunger away. It was sausage in an English muffin with egg, cold orange juice, two hash brown patties, one miniature cinnamon roll, a miniature chocolate croissant, and hot coffee with two little pods of cream. I took a picture for my blog. I tried to be simply in vacation mode, but I knew I couldn't help it. I needed to blog about this food when I got home. My frayed nerves slowly returned to semi-normal after a few bites of warm food.

When breakfast was over, I told Tony I wanted to walk around and take pictures of everything since it was my last twenty-four hours here. He told me to have fun and take my time. He needed to run a few errands and said he would catch up with me later.

I took pictures of the lounge where all the activities were, including the food court, the exercise room, the gift shop, the candy and chocolate shop, the children's playroom, and registration. I took pictures of the high ceilings with floating assorted fishes hanging on a wire as if they were swimming. I took pictures of the assorted candies and chocolates in large stemware glasses. I motioned for the cooks to stand close together, side by side and told them to say cheese. They proudly stood by the dessert table and smiled.

As I walked past the registration desk, a banner caught my attention. It said in bold black letters, GET MARRIED IN THE

MALDIVES. I asked the helper at the desk, and she assured me that it was true. They had a marriage scheduled for today even. She informed me that a priest from England lived locally by appointment and married couples. I thanked her and continued my self-guided tour. Getting married at the Maldives. It was refreshing but also terrifying. Those little "I do's" would change your circumstances and lives forever. But if I was ever to get married again, this is where I'd want to do it.

I took pictures of the white sofas with large pillows for backing and the lounge chairs with a square of glass at your feet, that looked directly into the ocean. The ceiling fans whirling overhead didn't make a sound, and the long jellyfish decorations weren't disturbed. A conference room was situated on the second floor with a long rectangular table with chairs for meetings.

I wandered back to my overwater bungalow where I glanced at my pool, checked the inside of my room, and left the front door open. I knew the thieves had been caught, but a speck of fear and cautiousness still hung with me, though that feeling was fading.

My last trip into the Maldives city was mostly sightseeing and visiting the jeweler. His shop had no customers, and he bowed his head in acknowledgement when he saw me enter. I went to the counter. I asked him if my earrings were ready, and he said they would be ready later today, and that he would bring them to me when they were ready. I explained that we had two other incidents with guys trying to steal the jewel from me. I told him that Tony had helped stop them, then security hauled them off in a police car, and they were apprehended and taken into custody. Ibrahim said he was very glad that everything had turned out alright and that I was safe.

As I was leaving, I told him that I had really enjoyed meeting him and that I considered him to be my friend.

"I'll see you again soon," he said, smiling. I waved goodbye.

Stopping by The Best Coffee, I picked up a chocolate cream cold brew, sat outside, and sipped my drink under the awning.

After returning to my bungalow, I decided on a white lacy top with a flowered skirt to wear with Tony tonight. I slipped into my bathtub for one last time. The vanilla bath bomb disintegrated under the flowing water. I closed my eyes and dreamed of being with Tony. How was I so fortunate to meet this man? I decided right there in the bathtub that it wasn't enough to find the perfect person, but in order to keep that love going, you had to be kind and work to keep that beautiful spark alive that attracted you to each other in the first place. I hoped I could do that with Tony for a long long time.

Tony seemed more happy than usual when he came to pick me up at 6:00pm. His kiss was not a grandma's peck on the cheek. His lips met mine with as much enthusiasm as mine met his. When we came up for air, he commented on my vanilla perfume. We were both breathing deeply when he said, "We'll be right on time for our dinner if we leave now." He grabbed my hand and led me along the boardwalk.

We walked to the aquarium hand in hand, past the informational room which explained the thick cut glass, past the other tourists taking a trip to the aquarium, down the stairs, moving from sunlight with every step to the land of the sea.

The restaurant was busy this evening with resort guests. It made sense that people would gather here for a special Christmas Eve dinner just like us. I was grateful and surprised once again that Tony was able to manage to get a reservation on such short notice. But now that I knew more about him, and imagined all the connections he had through his line of work, I guessed things like this worked out in his favor when he put his mind to them. We walked up to the restaurant entrance and were greeted by a cheerful hostess with a beautiful smile. She guided us to a table for two right next to the thick glass. It was close enough to touch. I placed my hand gently on its surface. It felt secure.

I was dazzled by the wildlife right before our eyes. Who gets the chance to see under the sea like this without scuba gear? It was extraordinary. Colorful schools of fish swam in unison, their scales shining iridescent in the light from the moon. A couple nurse sharks lazily swam along the ceiling of the glass dome did a U-turn, and swam back over us again. A few feet from my face was a large group of kissing fish. They swam right up to me as if to greet me then quickly darted away. I could hardly take my eyes away and look at the menu. I was completely enchanted.

The waiter came by and stood tall and professional in a white double-breasted uniform with black buttons as he explained our food choices. He described the wines, and I decided to have a rose Ferrari wine. Even though I didn't normally drink much, it was my last night here, and I wanted to celebrate. Tony went with Merlot. With my first sip, I knew I had chosen wisely. It was sharp and fresh, and it burned comfortingly in the back of my throat.

We ordered the Maldivian deep-fried egg rolls, with a bright orange sweet and sour sauce. Fancy miniature Parker house rolls with little pats of gold foiled butter accompanied it. As I was about to dip my egg roll in the sauce, a bright yellow puffer fish floated next to our table bringing along his companion, a blue spotted puffer fish. They slowed their swim to get a good glimpse of us.

"Tony, look at those puffer fish!" I said.

He looked up from his egg roll. "Those are pretty amazing."

"Tony, do you know there is actually a fish called the bastard mullet?"

He laughed. "Really?"

I nodded. "Another one that lives off the California coast is the sarcastic fringe head." We both laughed. I shook my head, still chuckling. The wine made everything seem funnier. "Who names these fish?"

"Speaking of names," Tony said. "Did you guess my middle name?"

I laughed. "No, but I have until the end of this fabulous meal to guess it. Maybe I will learn something else about you tonight that will give me a clue. I wanted to thank you, Tony. This is a once in a lifetime experience, and I am so honored to be sharing it with you, to have been invited by you. I never imagined when I first came to the Maldives that eating here was going to be possible for me. And here I am! The wonderful continuous floorshow of parading ocean life, the multi-flavored five-course meal, and being with you is the best Christmas gift I could possibly ask for."

"You're so welcome. I only wanted to bring my best gal to this place."

"Tony, I'm surprised you don't have another girlfriend. You are great fun, easy to be with, and I can't imagine another woman turning you down for anything."

I wrinkled my eyebrows and wondered at the appropriateness of those last two words. I didn't take it back because it was true. I went on, "With Jeff, I always had to second guess what I said. He would bring on these uncomfortable silences when I tried to be silly or be myself with him, and I never felt like I was enough for him. I worried sometimes that I was embarrassing to him or displeasing him in some way. He didn't share my sense of humor or my desire to have long conversations, or my need to have fun. But with you, I've never worried. I can be myself around you and say what I feel without fear of saying the wrong thing. It is so refreshing, and it makes me realize just what I gave up by staying married to Jeff for so long. I honestly thought that we probably had it as good as anyone else, so why try for something better? But with you, I realize things could have been so different."

Tony spoke slowly. "I have dated many women and most of them were very fine, but I was always looking for a particular type of woman, and I feel like I have found her in you."

Our waiter appeared carrying a large egg-shaped tray with our second dish. The hors d'oeuvres were a variety plate of small sausage fingers in a sweet barbecue sauce, cream cheese wontons, and thin ham slices wrapped in crispy bacon, held together with a toothpick. Two new plates were placed in front of us, while the used plates were cleared away.

I sampled a little of everything. So did Tony. The conversation went back to the women he'd dated.

"Have you ever met someone, and although you can't explain the reasons why, you know that something is missing? Don't get me wrong. They're all nice and fun, but there was no glue that held us together." Those words sounded familiar to me, so I stayed quiet to listen to what else he had to say about it.

"I wanted to be with someone that I not only loved, but someone who brought out the best in me. That is the kind of relationship that I saw my parents have, and I always knew that was special. I don't think everyone has that. I thought I had it with my first wife, but we didn't bring out the best in each other. We knew each other for so long that we never really considered other options. Even from the beginning, I think we both knew that there was something missing, but because of family pressure, we didn't want to admit it to ourselves. We weren't mad or miserable, but when we started to think of moving on, it started to feel better for both of us. She found in her new husband what she didn't find in me."

He stopped talking when the smiling waiter showed up with our small salads. He informed us that the salad was called boshi mashuni Maldivian salad. Served in a banana boat, the salad was made of sliced cabbage with coconut and banana flavors and spiced with curry, onions, and more spices with a chili pepper on top. I wanted to save room for the main entrée and dessert, so I ate a few bites and set my fork in the salad place.

"Tony, I know partly how you feel. I got this feeling that my marriage was wrong almost from the beginning, but one has to try over and over before you call it quits. I only felt that feeling of completeness that you are describing once, and it was when I was a little kid. It happened in just one day, so I'm not even sure if it was real, but it's the closest thing I can think of to what you are describing." Here I relayed a brief version of my experience with the boy at the park. "I never saw that kid again," I said.

Tony took a bite of his salad. He had that look on his face that he might say something profound. "That's pretty amazing that this kid had such a big effect on you," he said.

"Yeah, well he was a pretty amazing kid," I responded.

Tony did the wrinkled eyebrow thing again, and I waited for what he had to say. "Come to think of it, you are reminding me of a memory of my own when I was young. I sort of had a bit of the same experience when I was a kid."

"Really, what happened?"

"We played together as kids, just once. I remember really liking her," he seemed thoughtful. He looked at the fish swimming by and smiled as he thought back on the memory. "I also never saw her again."

"That's really sad and sweet," I said. "What happened? What was her name?"

"I think it was Tamera." He answered. "I was playing at a park by my grandparents' house. My sister and I were staying with them for a week while my parents were out of town. I was riding the merry-go-round. I stopped the merry-go-round and this girl got on. She had on a cool t-shirt and such a pretty smile. I remember that. She hopped on, and I pushed it faster and faster. When she spun around, I asked her what her name was. I was pretty sure she said Tamera or something, but she was going pretty fast, and her hair was flying."

I stopped eating my salad. The words Tony had just said were slowly sinking into my brain. The waiter arrived with the entrée and placed in front of me salmon with dill sauce and asparagus spears. Prime rib was Tony's choice, also with roasted asparagus.

Instead of picking up my fork to taste the salmon, I folded my arms in front of me and stared at Tony.

"Wait a minute. You met this girl on the playground, and she screamed out from the merry-go-round that her name was Tamera? Where was this? When was this?"

He nodded. "Oh it was a long time ago. I was probably 9 or 10 years old. It was in Georgia. I remember I played with this girl all afternoon. Then I had to beat up a bully that picked on her. When she drove away, I felt really sad, but I thought I might see her again if I came to that park."

I asked him, "How would you see her again?" My mind was racing. I stabbed my fork into the flakey salmon. When I bit into it, I hardly tasted it.

"Well, she told me she was there for a family reunion or something. They did it every year. This meat is very good and tender. Would you like a bite? Try some horseradish sauce with it."

I couldn't think of food. I could only think of what Tony was saying. My whole focus was on the experience Tony had when he was a child with a girl named Tamera.

I sat with my salmon untouched and took a deep breath. Tony's story was so familiar. But I was pretty sure the name of the boy who helped me was Dean. I would have remembered if his name was Tony because my family's dog's name was Tony. And then obviously my name is not Tamera. Another hitch. Could he have misheard the girl say her name that day as she was breezing by on the merry-go-round?

Or was it another girl at another park at another time all together on another merry-go-round? Besides, the odds of meeting that boy again as an adult in my present newly single state were just too astronomical. Weren't they?

His voice interrupted my train of thought. "Anyway, like I said, I never saw her again. I asked my mom to let us go back to that park hoping I'd meet her again, but we moved shortly after that, so I never did go back."

I felt a little dizzy. I excused myself and went to the restroom.

I looked at myself in the mirror and reapplied my lipstick thinking things over. It couldn't be. The facts in our stories were very similar, but our names weren't the same.

I wandered back to our table and tore off a piece of flaky salmon, squeezed a wedge of lemon on it, and dipped it in the tartar dill sauce. It was delicious and I ate three more bites and sipped my wine. Tony reached over and tried my salmon, giving it a thumbs up. That was also something new to me. Jeff never liked sharing food. I appreciated the gesture of intimacy.

"Quick question, Tony." I said

"Sure," he said.

"I don't know how to say this."

"Shoot," he said.

"By any chance in the entire Universe, is your middle name Dean? I know it doesn't match the S and 7 letters qualifications, but I just wondered."

His head popped up. He gave me a puzzled look. "How did you know about the name Dean? That's part of my middle name which I went by as a kid."

"You were known by Dean as a kid?" I asked, my heart thumping.

"Yeah, later I went by my given name."

What on earth? My mind was going crazy.

He asked me again. "How did you know about the name Dean?"

I took a long sip of wine.

"Well, you probably won't believe this, but I played with a kid named Dean at a family reunion. I was pretty little at the time."

"Wow, that's quite a coincidence," he said with a furrowed brow. He seemed to be thinking along the same lines as me. He explained, "I did go by Dean when I was young. I changed it back to Tony because it was easier to go by my first name."

Our dessert arrived just then. I tried the dessert. The decadent chocolate mousse cake melted in my mouth. It was worth waiting through the five-course dinner. And the chocolate gave me courage to continue.

"I don't know how to tell you this, but I'll try. When I was a young kid, I went to a family reunion."

Tony put his fingers up to his chin and watched me closely.

"I met this kid named Dean. We played for a long time and became friends. After this other blond kid poured sand on my head, Dean chased the bully down and made him come back and apologize. Then Dean rubbed my hair with the clean running water and brushed sand off my shoulders. I don't remember much else, but I really liked him and wanted to marry him. I was just a little kid." I laughed.

I looked at Tony. He looked perplexed.

"This can't really be happening, can it? I mean I have the same story to tell, as you do, only the girl's name was Tamera," Tony said.

"I think I have an explanation for that. I am wondering if when I shouted my name, I was going so fast on the merry-go-round, and you had never heard the name Tanna before, so you might have thought I said Tamera."

"I thought she said Tamera, but you're probably right. I had never heard the name Tanna before. I guess it could have been Tanna. I guess my little kid's brain figured it was Tamera." I could see the wheels turning in his head. He looked up at me and gave me a big smile.

"I need to take a quick stop at the restroom. I'll be right back," he said. He squeezed my shoulder as he passed.

As I watched him walk away, a surprising and euphoric feeling came over me. Could it really be him? What would he say when he came back? Did he go to the restroom to try and wrap his head around it? How was this going to play out? My excitement was overwhelming.

As he slid back into his seat, I noticed a smile on his face. Did he feel the same as I did? "Is it really you?" he asked. "And if it is really you—I hope to the moon and back again that it is you—I just have a question for you. Did you ever go back to the reunion?"

"Yeah, I did. My mom and dad took us every year after that first year, for a few years, … Dean." I wondered how he'd react to me calling him his childhood name.

His eyes widened. "I haven't been called that for a long time."

"Tanna, this is a pretty special moment for me. I can't even believe this happened here in the Maldives. Who would ever have thought? I mean, here we are, both single, both on vacation, and here we meet each other again after all this time. Like you, I wanted to find you all my life."

He looked up as if to thank heaven above. My hands trembled. We both just looked at each other smiling. "I think now is a good time as ever to tell you my middle name," he said breaking the spell.

"Well, it's about time."

"Are you ready for this? Drum roll please."

"I'm ready." I drummed my fingers on the table laughing feeling as light as air.

"My middle name actually comes from my mom's grandfather. She knew him as a little girl and loved his name. I think my great-grandpa and I are probably the only two people that have had this name."

He paused for dramatic effect.

"It's Sandean. Anthony Sandean Roberts," he said.

"Sandean. That's beautiful. It starts with S, ends with N, and has seven letters. That checks off the boxes." I smiled. "Well, I didn't guess it, so you can keep your firstborn. You win." I bowed as genteelly as I could while sitting down.

"Well, Tanna/Tamera. Let me ask you a question."

I held my breath.

Tony stood up and pulled his chair over to my side so he was sitting beside me. He put his hand over mine. "Since I have found the girl of my dreams, and it took me long enough. I have something I want to tell you."

His thumb traced circles on my hand. "Tanna, when I came here this evening, I had made a decision. I found you. You are that second star that I was destined to meet again. I didn't know you were that little girl on the playground I always wanted to marry. I thought you were the closest thing to her, but miracle of miracles, you are her." He took a breath. "Do you remember that I made you a counteroffer if you won? Well, even though I won, I want to still offer myself to you. I hope you will take me as your friend and as a husband."

My hands immediately covered my face as my bottom lip started to tremble, and tears came into my eyes. I tried not to sob out loud so as not to disturb the other restaurant guests. Tony put his arms around me. I turned my head and sobbed into his shirt. He held me close. With my eyes closed, I found my napkin and dabbed my eyes.

I had found the love of my life after all those years. With his arms around me, I was transported back in time. I watched two young kids on the playground swings, not flying high in the air, but talking, slowly pushing themselves back and forth in unison with their feet, and knowing that there was no place on earth they would rather be. That was how I felt now—there was no place on earth I would rather be.

"So here's my question," Tony said. "Will you take me? Will you marry me? You know we haven't known each other all that long," he trailed off seeming suddenly unsure of himself.

A JEWEL IN THE MALDIVES

"I beg to differ," I assured him in my shaking voice. "I have known you for over four decades."

His smile grew brighter if that was possible. "So will you marry me?"

I suddenly thought of my family back home and the life I had and a wave of doubt washed over me. *What would I tell my kids? They will have a screaming fit because we've only known each other for a short time. What would I tell my parents? They will think we are crazy and that it's just infatuation. And what about our jobs? Who will relocate and where will we live?* The questions flooded my mind and made me hesitate. "The answer is maybe."

He pulled away puzzled and looked at my face. "Maybe?" His face fell slightly.

In the past, I had been immobilized, not able to move or make even a small decision. Those feelings had resurfaced. I remembered my dream running through the dark cave away from the tiger and how scared I felt. It took me a minute to realize that I was not that little girl anymore, or even the newly divorced middle-aged woman anymore, fearful about every decision, scared of what people might think or say. Just like in the dream, I knew this was my moment to take a leap of faith. Due to all the experiences leading up to now, I knew I could change the course of my thinking.

I was an adult woman and much more confident. I knew I loved this man and wanted to be with him. I felt a surge of empowerment come over me. Did it really matter what my kids thought? My parents would surely have objections, but I had a strong feeling they would love him too. Our jobs could be tailored to how we liked. Every single thought that I saw as problems could be worked out. All that really mattered was we had found each other and that after meeting so long ago, we were able to start our lives together.

"You know, whatever else I'm worried about doesn't hold a candle to being with you. It will all work out. I know it will, and I'm getting better at not being scared anymore. I'm trying to develop the courage to move forward and make good decisions. So, Tony," I took his face in my hands and looked into his eyes, "With all my heart, my answer is yes!"

His face lit up like a firework. And he kissed me. There was applause from onlookers at the restaurant. We broke apart and smiled at everyone. "Whew, that's a relief," he said. A sneaky smile broke across his face. "If you hadn't said yes, I don't know what I would have done with this little gift."

He reached into his pocket and brought out a small white jewelry box. He turned the box so that its opening faced me. He raised the lid.

"Oh, my heavens above!" I exclaimed.

There was a familiar large pink stone in the middle with little diamonds surrounding it, which he placed on the fourth finger of my left hand.

"Is this the jewel? I thought Ibrahim was making it into earrings for me."

"Yes," he said. "He was, but I talked him out of it and convinced him to make this instead as a surprise to you."

"It's so beautiful, Tony." My arms automatically went around his neck, and I kissed him again.

Our waiter showed up and cleared his throat to announce his presence. I thrust my left hand up to his face to show him my ring.

"I offer my sincerest congratulations to the happy couple!" he said. "Will there be anything else for you two tonight?"

"No, I think that's all," Tony said.

We walked out of the restaurant and up the stairs with his arm around my shoulders and my arm around his waist.

Chapter 22

As we stood in the registration area, Tony said, "If you hadn't said yes, all of my other plans for the evening would have to be canceled."

"What other plans?" I inquired.

Tony held up his hand high in the air and appeared to be searching the guests for someone. He waved.

Abbey jogged toward us with Marina following behind. I could see her parents walking fast to keep up. Abbey slammed into me with a giant hug.

"Let me see your ring!" she screamed. I showed it to her. "Oh, it's so pretty. Are those real diamonds?"

"They sure are," Tony said.

"It's really pretty," Abbey said. "Pink's my favorite color."

"Mine too," I said.

Abbey's parents reached out to shake our hands.

I noticed that Abbey and Marina were wearing little pink flower crowns on their heads. "Those are pretty crowns," I said. "Why are you wearing them?"

Abbey gave me a knowing smile. "That's the secret I couldn't tell you." Then she looked at Tony.

He took a deep breath. "You know how you agreed to marry me? Well, can we do it sooner rather than later?"

My heart thumped. "How much sooner?"

I was starting to get the full picture and why the girls were wearing pretty little flower girl crowns.

"Is now a good time?" he asked taking my hand.

"Right now?" I took a deep breath.

I turned to Tony. "I'd love to get married to you right now and have these two darlings be the flower girls."

Abbey and Marina jumped up and down like they had springs in their shoes. Their enthusiasm was contagious.

Tony turned to the small family. "Will you excuse us for a moment? We will be right back."

We walked toward the registration desk, and a man who appeared to be a priest smiled at us with papers in his hands.

Tony introduced me to Father Andrew who would be marrying us. Father Andrew had a few words of instruction before the wedding. He informed us that our wedding would not be legally binding, although it was still a formal ceremony. Once we returned home, we could officially get married and make the wedding legal. He told us many couples get married in the Maldives, then return home and have a legal ceremony with family and friends. The idea of having my children attend the wedding back home would be the only way I would want it. So that was something to look forward to when we returned home.

I turned to Tony and said, "So this is what you've been doing when you said you had a few things to do, like planning a wedding?"

"Yes, ma'am. I'm very efficient." He winked, and my heart melted.

We walked toward Sarah and Dustin and the girls. Sarah handed me a beautiful crown made of tropical flowers that she placed on my head like a tiara. I felt like a princess and thanked her. Tony introduced Father Andrew to Abbey's family.

Tony explained to everyone that the church officiate was here from England, so he had made an appointment with him.

My mind was whirling faster than the merry-go-round from our childhood. The next surprise was Ibrahim, the jeweler from town. He walked right up to us. "Congratulations!" he said. "I wouldn't miss this for the world."

Right behind him was the security guard and the baker from the chocolate sweets and candy shop carrying a tray with an eight-inch-round six-layer chocolate cake with caramel and ganache topping, napkins and forks and small paper plates.

I turned to Tony. "Where will we be married?"

He pointed. "Right over there." I could see the little walk to the pier with white lights decorating the gazebo at the end. *So that's my wedding chapel.*

Tony thanked everyone for coming, then turned to me. "Shall we?" I looked down at my dress. I didn't feel appropriately dressed for such an occasion, but I decided it didn't matter. I was marrying the man of my dreams, and I could always look at wedding dresses back in California for the legal wedding.

We all walked toward the pier. A glorious Christmas tree stood to the size of the gazebo strung with beautiful lights. The gazebo was adorned in garlands and holly. It was a tropical Christmas wonderland. I couldn't think of a more ideal setting. The little girls picked rose petals from their baskets and tossed them on the ground with every step they took. We all took our places, and the preacher stepped forward.

The ceremony was short and simple. He told us that we had a wonderful chance of being very happy. He said now that we had found the right person, we should always be kind and never take each other for granted. That is something I would not do. I would always be grateful that I had come to the Maldives and met my beloved again to have a second chance with him. Then the priest pronounced us husband and wife in front of these witnesses.

A small crowd seemed gathered on the boardwalk and were snapping photos. We smiled when we noticed a phone was turned in our direction, but the joy I felt inside a camera could never capture. We were married. We kissed like we were drinking water for the first time after a long dry spell, and I could hear cheers from the crowd.

When we broke apart, we were surrounded by our well-wishers. Someone from the resort even rolled out a "Just Married" banner, and music started playing in the background. Everyone in attendance showered us with flower petals. We hugged our friends. The people passing by at the other end of the pier clapped and cheered. I could hear a few whistles and bells chimed. A photographer had come by and photographed our special moment. Tony and I held onto each other as we gathered everyone around us for more pictures.

A cake was rolled out and cut into small triangle-shaped pieces and served to our wedding party. Ibrahim gifted us a beautiful wreath with tropical flowers to symbolize our forever union. We thanked everyone in attendance including Abbey and her family, the baker, the security guard, and the priest. He handed us our marriage license.

"You seem like a truly wonderful couple. I wish you all the best."

"Thank you and thank you for officiating at our wedding," Tony said.

All the wedding guests slowly walked back to the open-air building. Each congratulated us and went in different directions.

I motioned for Dustin and Sarah and the little girls to come and sit for a moment. "Want to know something, Abbey?"

"Yeah, sure."

"Tony and I just found out tonight that we knew each other as children. We were at a playground when we were little, and we met each other and really liked each other."

"Really? Oh wow, that's a good love story," Sarah chimed.

I looked over at my little friend. "Abbey, I want to thank you for being a good friend to me and all of your family. I had no idea I'd meet such wonderful people on my trip to the Maldives. I thought

I would spend Christmas alone, but thanks to all of you," I looked lovingly at Tony and all my friends, "I had the most wonderful vacation and tomorrow will be the best Christmas I could ever ask for."

"I'm so glad we got to be friends," Abbey said. "I'll write to you."

"Me too," Marina piped in.

Tony and I gave her a thumbs-up. We gave everyone hugs again, and we separated so the girls could get to bed.

Tony and I sat alone. We didn't talk. We only sat, basking in the glow of each other's company. This is where I wanted to be, to sit with him, married to him. I remembered my dream from the flight over here.

"Tony, I had a dream when I first came to the Maldives about a man who was tall, dark, and handsome."

"Oh yeah? That would be me." He laughed.

"Tony, I can't believe these surprising last few hours. They have been some of the best hours of my life." I held up my left hand and examined my wedding ring.

"For me too. Oh, speaking of dreams, by the way, do you remember that dream I had when the two stars were rising in the sky and heading toward each other?"

"Yeah, I do. Did they ever get together?"

"Yes, they did. They are together now and shining bright as one."

"That's so sweet. It's us, isn't it?"

"Yes. It's us."

"You know what this feels like?" I said.

"Let me guess," he said. "Does it feel like we never missed a beat, and we just picked up as if we had never been apart?"

"Wow," I said. "You took the words from my mouth. Even though it feels like that, I feel like we have a lot of catching up to do. I can't wait to spend the rest of my life catching up with you."

We sat for a few more minutes until the hard wood on the bench felt like it was about to burrow into our bones. I turned to Tony. "Which bungalow are we going to tonight, yours or mine?"

He turned to me and said, "Well, neither one."

I asked. "Oh, are we spending the night under the stars?"

"No, but close." He paused. I waited.

"We are going to spend our first night together under the ocean," he said.

I stood up and put my hands on the sides of his face and kissed him. "I love you so much."

I looked up. "And thank you, Universe."

He laughed. "So how fast can you pack your bags?"

"So get engaged, get married, and honeymoon under the sea all in one evening?"

"Yup, that's the order of things."

"You remember I'm a quick-change artist, don't you? I can also pop my clothes into my suitcase at the same speed. Those clothes will fly in like the police were after them."

We started walking back to our bungalows hand in hand ready for the next big adventure, which would begin under the sea on Christmas in the Maldives.

The End

About the Author

Raised in the small town of Tabiona, Utah, Katherine Bell was always looking for her next big adventure. Her dad fostered her love of adventure by taking her to hunt for rocks and for ancient, Native American beads. She loved the thrill and mystery of these treasure hunts.

After taking an English writing class in college, writing stories became one of her passions. As she raised her family, she told stories to her children every night. Today, she still enjoys sharing stories and making memories with her growing family including four children and twelve grandchildren.

Katherine loves the ocean and especially savors any opportunity to connect with the water, the waves, and the lightly salted air of Southern California beaches. She is passionate about food and considers herself a foodie, much like her main character in *A Jewel in the Maldives*. She also plays the piano–including at church and improv piano on a baby grand at home. This is her debut novel, inspired in large part by the encouragement of her daughter, a poet and a fellow writer.

For more, please visit:

www.MerryRobinPublishing.com/KatherineBell

We would love to hear your feedback in the form of a review on Amazon.com and/or Goodreads. Small efforts such as leaving a review, sharing with a friend and requesting this book at your local library make a world of difference for authors!

Thank you

www.ingramcontent.com/pod-product-compliance
Lightning Source LLC
Chambersburg PA
CBHW032003240626
47153CB00003B/1108